Ox-Tales
WATER

*Original stories from
remarkable writers*

Ox-Tales are published in support of

 **Oxfam**

First published in Great Britain in 2009 by *Green*Profile, an imprint of
Profile Books Ltd, 3A Exmouth House, Pine Street, London EC1R 0JH

Printed in the UK by CPI Bookmarque, Croydon, CR0 4TD
Typeset in Iowan to a design by Sue Lamble

1 3 5 7 9 10 8 6 4 2

A CIP catalogue record for this book is
available from the British Library

ISBN: 978 1 84668 260 5

Mixed Sources
Product group from well-managed
forests and other controlled sources
www.fsc.org Cert no. TT-COC-002227
© 1996 Forest Stewardship Council
FSC

Ox-Tales: Water

OX-TALES: WATER is one of four original collections, featuring stories by leading British- and Irish-based writers. Each of the writers has contributed their story for free in order to raise money and awareness for Oxfam. The FOUR ELEMENTS provide a loose framework for the stories and highlight key areas of Oxfam's work: water projects (WATER), aid for conflict areas (FIRE), agricultural development (EARTH), and action on climate change (AIR). An afterword, at the end of each book, explains how Oxfam makes a difference. And in buying this book, you'll be a part of that process, too.

Compiling these books, we asked authors for new stories; or, from novelists who don't do short stories, work in progress from their next book. The response was thirty-eight original pieces of fiction, which are spread across the four books and framed by a cycle of element poems by Vikram Seth. We think they're extraordinary, but be your own judge. And if you like what you read here, please buy all four OX-TALES books – and help Oxfam work towards an end to poverty worldwide.

Mark Ellingham (Profile) & Peter Florence (Hay Festival)
Editors, OX-TALES

Acknowledgments

The Ox-Tales books were developed at Profile Books by Mark Ellingham in association with Peter Florence and Hay Festival. Thanks from us both to the authors who contributed stories – and time – to creating these four collections in support of Oxfam. And thanks, too, to their publishers and agents who, without exception, offered generous support to this project.

At Oxfam, Tom Childs has guided the project alongside Suzy Smith, Charlie Hayes, Annie Lewis, Fee Gilfeather, Annemarie Papatheofilou and Matt Kurton.

At Profile, Peter Dyer, Penny Daniel, Niamh Murray, Duncan Clark, Claire Beaumont, Simon Shelmerdine, Ruth Killick, Rebecca Gray, Kate Griffin and Andrew Franklin have been instrumental. Thanks also to Nikky Twyman and Caroline Pretty for proofreading, and to Jonathan Gray for his cover illustrations.

Contents

VIKRAM SETH (born Calcutta, India, 1952) is the author of the novels *The Golden Gate* (1986), *A Suitable Boy* (1993) and *An Equal Music* (1999), and of books of poetry, travel, fable and memoir.

'Water' is part of a sequence of poems, *Seven Elements*, incorporating the elements in the European, Indian and Chinese traditions (earth, air, fire, water, wood, metal and space). Set to music by the composer Alec Roth, *Seven Elements* will be performed in summer 2009 at the Salisbury, Chelsea and Lichfield festivals.

Water

The moon bobs in the river's spate.
The water's deep, the waves are wide.
Around my house lie springtime floods.
My friend and I drink tea inside.

Du Fu is singing at the mast.
Li Bai lies in his watery grave.
Far far away, on alien shores
The lashing breakers mourn and rave.

The hermit sits upon the ice.
The ice-bear moves from floe to floe
And from the hot spring newly bathed
Snow monkeys roll upon the snow.

The clouds disperse, the ropes thaw out.
Ice tinkles down from frozen sails.
The ocean churns and treasures rise:
Ambrosia and minke whales.

Slivers of ice brush past my face
As I swim in the icy bay.
A rumbling glacier calves a berg.
The watery sun shoots forth a ray.

The turbined vessel steams and steers
But cannot veer around the ice.
The beavers build but cannot dam
The stream that flows through Paradise.

Water destroys the unbaked pot.
Water is magicked into wine.
Water dissolves the fabled salt
And sinks the lover in the Rhine.

If only I were wine instead
Of water and my breath a cloud,
Of man's last disobedience and
This brittle world I'd sing aloud.

O water-being, drunk with gain,
Mere water are your brains and blood
And water are your flesh and tears
And water is the coming flood.

The ice-caps melt, the ports are drowned.
The current from the gulf is still.
The darkening planet drinks the sun
And cyclones swirl and whirl and kill.

Where are the islands of delight?
Where are the fields that now are dust?
Where is the crop of measured years?
I weep, I weep because I must.

My friend and I drink tea and wine.
Upon the pane our breath is steam.
Our tears flow down from grief and joy.
We dream and drink, we drink to dream.

Vikram Seth

Rice Cakes and Starbucks

ESTHER FREUD (born London, 1963) trained as an actress at the London Drama Centre before writing *Hideous Kinky*, the first of six novels to date, the most recent of which is *Love Falls* (2007). Her story 'Rice Cakes and Starbucks' is part of a work in progress, which will emerge as a novel, *Lucky Break*, in 2010.

WHEN THE LINDENS ARRIVED in Los Angeles it was raining. Not drizzling, or even pouring, but streaming down outside the glass doors of the departure lounge in thick, grey sideways slices. Water sluiced along the airport roads, tumbling in the gutters, spinning in the wheels of the taxis that splashed up to collect the lucky people at the head of the queue.

Dan and Beth stood and stared out through the sheets of glass. 'Blimey,' they said, almost in unison, and Dan put his hand up to his mouth and laughed.

'I'm cold,' their eldest child, Honey, shivered in her pink T-shirt and Dan knelt down to rifle through the bags, removing as he did so numerous insubstantial outfits which they'd packed with the expectation of the five of them, lifted out of a grey London morning into an endless bright blue Californian afternoon.

Dan and Beth had rented a house in the hills. The house had been recommended by a friend of Dan's, although at the last minute his wife had interjected: They can't stay up there! They've got to be by the ocean. In Santa Monica.

'But Santa Monica's extortionate, and you don't even get a pool,' Dan's friend had told her, 'and what's the point of LA if there's no pool?'

Beth and Dan had listened nervously. They'd already said yes to the house in the hills, paid their deposit, filled in numerous forms for insurance, gas, electrics and telephone, and so neither of them mentioned Santa Monica or the ocean again. Instead they talked about the pool. 'The pool, the pool,' they repeated like a charm and the children tugged on their swimming costumes, blew up their armbands and ran shrieking down the draughty, carpeted stairs of their north London home.

The higher they drove, the more heavily it rained. It clattered on the roof of the taxi and washed in sheets over the windscreen, and occasionally when the driver stopped to call the number they gave him for directions they could see the water rushing past them downhill over the cobbled streets. 'Got it,' he assured their landlord, who was waiting with the key, but then almost immediately they became lost again, roaring along narrow roads, catching glimpses of lit-up Spanish villas and rain-soaked ferns and the same few street names over and over again.

By the time they found the house, in a tiny cul-de-sac obscured by darkness and a large half-fallen bush, Ben and the baby were asleep, although Honey was still up, staring out intently at the night. 'Careful,' the driver warned as Dan stepped into a foot of gushing water, and the landlord opened the yard door and stood watching them from underneath a white umbrella as they struggled with their luggage and the warm weights of their children, unloading them into the chilled hush of the hall.

It had been Beth's idea to come. 'Dan!' he'd heard her calling from the bathroom, and although she hated it when the children shouted to her from the top of the house, she was doing it herself now. 'DAN!'

Slowly he walked upstairs and put his head round the door. 'What is it?' He waited. She was lying stretched out in the bath, her face flushed, her hair a straggle of curls, her breasts still swollen and veined from feeding Grace. 'What?'

'I've been thinking. We could rent this house out, say for six months, put all our things in storage, and then, before the children get too big, we could go to America and give it a chance. While your series is still on.'

Dan sat down on the toilet seat.

'We could get good money for this house,' she continued. 'And we could use that money to rent something nice out there.'

Dan looked at his feet. He felt unutterably guilty. 'We could,' he nodded as if he was taking it seriously. 'Yes, we could.'

Beth was busy calculating. 'I'll phone the estate agent first thing on Monday and see what they say. And we could look into the right time to go. If there's a good time, a good season ...'

'I don't think they have seasons.'

'Don't they have pilot season?'

'Well, yes ...'

Honey was shouting from the kitchen. A door slammed and Ben gave an almighty scream. Dan imagined fingers caught in hinges, tiny creased digits sliced right off. He flew down the stairs. 'What are you doing?' Honey and Ben looked round at him. They'd climbed onto the worktop to get at some biscuits and for a second they froze.

'No,' he snatched the biscuits away. 'It's lunch soon.' And then thinking that actually, with Beth still in the bath and the baby sleeping, lunch may not be for several hours, he peeled back the shiny plastic wrapping and gave them a biscuit each. 'Just one,' he said, to impress upon them the inflexibility of this new rule.

'Oh please, just two?' Honey made her grey eyes round as coins, and giving up any pretence he was in charge Dan slid out two more and shoved them into their hot hands.

'Dan!' Beth was shouting to him again.

Wearily he trudged back upstairs. 'What?'

'Shall we do it?' Her eyes were gleaming.

'I don't know.'

'Why not?' she challenged, and instead of telling her why not – so that he could blame her forever, for holding him back, for having three children when he only needed one, for making it impossible to realise his dreams when they all relied on him, all four of them, to be at home, he changed the inflection and shrugged. 'Why not?'

They looked at each other and Dan attempted a smile. 'I mean, the worst thing that can happen is that they hate me, and then we can come home.'

'Well, not if we've rented out the house.'

'True.' Dan bit his lip. 'Well, they'll just have to love me.'

'They *do* love you. Didn't Finola say the show was getting great reviews?' And showering him with tiny flicks of water Beth levered herself out.

The house was immaculately furnished, with fragile lamps and highly polished surfaces, and although it had a den, a dressing room and a study, it seemed to only have one bedroom. 'But it does have a pool,' Beth said brightly, and they pressed their noses against the black panes of glass and stared out into its choppy, rectangular depth.

All night it rained. Dan could hear it crashing against the glass windows of their cold white room while Grace kicked and snuffled in the bed between them and Ben and Honey shifted uneasily on lilos that they'd lain down in the dressing room next door. At three Grace woke and began to gurgle happily as if it were late morning, which of course it was, for her, and Dan turned on his side and pretended to be oblivious. Beth fed her and shushed her and even pleaded a little with her to be quiet and then, sighing, got up and took her away. Not long after, he heard Ben begging to be allowed to go in the pool, and then Honey screaming that she was mean, mean, mean for not letting them even try it. 'It's dark,' Beth protested, remarkably cheerfully, and some time later, although it was *still* dark, he heard the garden door creak open and the sounds of the three of them, Beth, Honey and Ben, squealing as they ran out into the rain to dip their feet into the water. 'It's freezing!' Honey complained. 'You said it would be warm!' And he heard the slam of the door as they hurtled back in.

Eventually when he really was asleep, Beth slid in beside him. Her body was chilled, and he jolted unpleasantly as she pressed herself against his back for warmth. 'Grace is having a nap and the others are watching *Sponge Bob*,' she whispered, and Dan tried to remember where he was. Oh God, it all came back to him. What if they don't like me? What if I can't get a single audition, let alone a job, and then by the time I get back to London they've forgotten who I am? He felt so sick and miserable that when the baby woke from her nap, forty minutes later, Beth had to kick him in the shins to rouse him.

But once Dan was in the kitchen with Grace under one arm, he was cheered by the sheer Americanness of every-thing. The size of the fridge, inside which was a two-litre carton of fresh orange juice and a giant bag of bagels, the size of the cooker with its industrial grey hob, and the sheer width of the widescreen television before which his chil-dren sat like puppies, their eyes round, their mouths open. He peered out at the pool. It filled every available space of garden and could be reached from French doors in the den. Once it stops raining, Dan told himself, I'll swim in that pool every day, one hundred lengths, until my body is hard and lean and employable.

But it didn't stop raining. 'Is this normal?' they asked the landlord, who appeared shortly after nine to tell them how to work the washing machine and the dryer, how to sweep out the gas-fuelled log fire, and adjust the temperature in the pool when – if ever – that became applicable.

'Not normal at all.' He shook his head and he flicked on the television news to show them how some of the neighbouring houses, clinging to the hill by steps and stilts, were beginning to slide down the mountain. 'Four people out there already lost their lives,' he said. 'And this rain's still not letting up.'

He lent them his umbrella and offered to drive Dan to a car hire centre.

'I won't be long.' He turned to Beth, who'd been mentioning since seven that it would be great to get out, somewhere, anywhere, for breakfast, or lunch, or whatever meal they were on now.

'Dan …' she hissed, widening her eyes at him, but he pretended not to notice and quickly turned away. 'I'll be half an hour at the most.'

The car hire centre was clean and spacious. There were large gleaming saloons and magnificent four-by-fours. 'I need a family car, with a baby seat, and a booster seat … Do I get a discount if I take it for …', he swallowed, 'a while?'

'You sure do.' The man smiled at him, his teeth so white they were opaque. And by the time he'd chosen and filled in all the forms, the car salesman, whose name was Duane, had wished him not just a Nice Day, but a Fantastic Day, with such genuine enthusiasm that Dan felt quite uplifted. Once behind the wheel, he couldn't resist it, he took the car for a quick spin, and then finding himself driving past a supermarket he decided to stop and buy provisions. The supermarket was enormous – a whole aisle for sliced cheese! And after filling his basket with fruit and vegetables he became distracted by the hardware section, where he bought cheap raincoats, a pack of cards, and a teething ring for the baby. Then on the way back he forgot the street sign was hidden by the fallen bush and drove fast past it at least five times. When he finally arrived home it was after twelve.

'How is everyone?' He rushed in through the rain, shaking himself and stamping in the hall.

Beth's face was stony. 'Fine.' She handed him the baby and slammed out of the room.

'What's up with Mummy?' he asked in a conspiratorial way, and Honey hung her head and said Mummy was cross because she'd taken Grace into the garden. 'I only dipped her feet in the pool up to her toes. I wanted to see if she'd like it.'

'And did she like it?' Dan lay the baby along the length of his knees and kissed the dense pads of her socked feet.

'Not really. I think it's too cold for her. She screamed and screamed and cried.'

'Right.' Beth was back. She looked as if she'd been crying too. 'Let's go. We need to get out of this house. Now.'

'For God's sake.' Beth frowned when she saw the car. A great black SUV that all three children had to be lifted into.

Dan raised his hands to show the decision had been beyond him. 'It's all they had,' he told her. 'And if it goes on raining we'll need something powerful to get us up and down this goddamn mountain ...'

'Sure, sure ...' Beth threw him a disbelieving look as she climbed into the front.

The inside of the car smelled so new, so sleek and shiny, that it made Dan smile. The windscreen wipers whipped back and forth, the lights on the dashboard twinkled. 'Hang on,' he said and he ran back into the house and returned with a CD which he slipped into the player. Green Day swelled and roared above the weather. The children squealed and even Beth couldn't resist a smile. 'Where to?' he asked, as if everything, from now on, was up to her.

'Let's just drive around and find somewhere nice to eat.' There was a map in the glove compartment and Beth stretched it over her lap. 'Sunset Boulevard,' she read.

'Really?' Dan peered out.

'No. I just had to say it.' She took a breath. 'Venice Beach.'

'You're confusing me.' Dan sped through a junction.

'Beverly Hills. West Hollywood.'

'Look, we're on Santa Monica Boulevard.' Dan pointed. 'Shall I keep going?'

Beth stared at the map. 'It leads right to the sea. That would be fun.'

An hour later they were still on Santa Monica Boulevard. The traffic stopped and started, grinding slowly forward in the rain. Dan kept his eyes open for a restaurant. Burger bars and fast food chains lined the deserted streets. 'I thought everyone was meant to be so healthy out here,' Beth squinted.

'Not everyone. Just Brad Pitt. Everyone else is fat as fuck.'

'Daddy!'

'Fat as a duck, I said.'

'How about there?' Beth pointed but it wasn't a restaurant at all; just an antique shop with a table laid for supper, rosebud crockery and a bowl of glass grapes. They drove on, the windscreen wipers working powerfully, Green Day playing over again.

The children were unusually quiet, stunned by the time change, the rain and the music. 'If we don't stop soon, they'll go to sleep,' Beth worried. 'And we'll all be up again tomorrow at 2am. Or some of us will.'

Dan turned off Santa Monica Boulevard and sped along smaller streets, crossing junctions and searching left and right, until with a screech of brakes he pulled up at a sign for pizza.

But it was too late. All three were fast asleep. Dan and Beth looked over at their children. Honey, with her halo of gold curls, her black lashes laying like a fan against her skin, Ben, his thick mouse tufts unbrushed for several days, one ear bright red where it had folded over against the seat, and the baby, Grace, still bald, her face unformed, a silver line of dribble hanging from her chin.

'Shall we go back to the house?' he said. 'I bought some food. We could make lunch there and then wake them up.'

They glanced at the pizza restaurant. A row of men in beige security uniforms sat at the window on stainless steel stools. 'Or not wake them?'

Beth slid her hand onto his knee. She lowered her voice to a sultry purr. 'We could have a quick sleep first.'

'Exciting.' Dan mimicked Ben's current favourite word, and more slowly, with the music lower, they drove home.

It was a week before Dan had his first casting. His American manager, Finola, called to say that things were Great. They were going Really Well. A lot of people had seen his series on BBC America and she'd been sending out his showreel, talking him up, and now, finally, he had a meeting with a casting woman from CBS. 'But how are you managing,' she asked, concerned, 'with your little ones, and all this rain?'

'Fine, fine,' Dan told her. 'We're used to it.'

But it wasn't true.

'What's the point of this place if it isn't sunny?' Beth shook her head, and Dan overheard her telling the baby, 'If it rains one more day, we're going home.' He didn't ask her how she planned to break the news to the Dutch osteopath and his family who'd rented their house for half a year, or to Finola, who swore she was working round the clock to get him seen. 'It wouldn't be so bad if it wasn't for the fucking pool,' she stormed. 'The children never let up for a moment, whining and pleading to be allowed to swim.'

'Just let them,' Dan muttered, but he had to agree that it was freezing, the surface of the pool awash with debris, palm fronds and the dried brown tendrils of a plant that looked like spiders.

The day of the casting Dan woke early. At first he imagined it must be nerves, but then he realised that it was silence that had woken him. The downpour had finally stopped and the window was filled with a thick grey rainless light. Miraculously the children were still sleeping: Grace, her warm pink face visible beneath Beth's arm; the others on their makeshift beds in the room next door. Very carefully he tiptoed into the kitchen. He took a breath. It was the first time in a week, the first time since the car hire centre, that he'd been alone. He opened the French doors and stepped out into the garden. The air smelled good. Musty and foreign. He knelt down and dipped his fingers in the pool. The water was still cold, but hopeful and intoxicating and above him hung one tall palm, its leaves a far-off flower.

Dan was startled by a shriek. 'We're going in!' There were Ben and Honey, tugging off their pyjamas, screaming and hopping with joy.

'Hang on, you two. It's only 6.45!' But Dan didn't have the heart to stop them.

'Don't move,' he said instead and he ran in and grabbed Ben's armbands, unpacked and waiting since the first day. As fast as he could he blew them up. Honey was in first. 'It's not cold!' she said defiantly, although her teeth were chattering. Ben screamed as he jumped, and then screamed louder and longer as he hit the water. 'It's not cold either,' he promised, once he'd recovered from the shock. Dan pulled a chair outside and watched them, ducking and fighting and flicking water at each other until their lips were blue.

Beth made porridge, although, like everything, it tasted different – finer, softer, further removed from the original oat. Her face was creased and heavy with a rare night of unbroken sleep. 'I think we're over the worst.' She rubbed the children's towelled bodies to bring back blood and she smiled hopefully at Dan.

After breakfast Dan tried on his suit. Did men wear suits in California? He didn't know, but he couldn't help admire himself in the charcoal cut of it. He moved back and forth before the mirror, sucking in his cheekbones, sticking out his chest, checking the imperfect creases of his trousers. 'No hands! No hands!' He warded off the children as they rushed towards him and he heard Beth sigh.

'I thought the meeting wasn't till twelve.'

'Yes. But I need to find it first. It's somewhere in West Hollywood and I thought I'd go for a coffee before ... get my bearings. Take stock.'

Beth handed him a muslin and then the baby, both of which he took reluctantly. 'I'm going to get a shower.'

As soon as she was back she dressed the children and then began to pack a bag. Rice cakes, water, tangerines, bananas.

'Where are you going?' Dan asked, still holding Grace, hardly daring to take his eye from her in case she threw up over his shoulder.

'I thought we'd come with you. We can find a Starbucks or something and wait.'

Dan was appalled. 'No ... really.' He imagined running from the flock of his children, scattering rice cakes and baby milk, muslins and Frappaccino, arriving red-faced and dishevelled at the marble steps of CBS.

'We can't stay here all day.' Beth didn't meet his eye. She didn't want an argument and they both knew she'd waver if she saw the fury in his face.

'Beth, it's why we came. For me to get work!'

'I know. I know.' She bustled at the sink, putting the porridge pan on to soak, wiping down the surfaces. 'But I can't spend another day in this house ...' she swallowed. 'No school. No nursery.'

Dan put Grace on the floor, where she sometimes could and sometimes couldn't stay upright on her own. She sat for a second and then fell forward, her face squashing into a rubber mat.

'Sweetheart.' He took hold of Beth's shoulders. 'I won't be gone all day. It's stopped raining now. You can take them for a walk or something.'

'Dan.' She looked at him and her face was white. 'What's

more important to you? An episode of *Entourage* or finding your wife and three children lying at the bottom of that pool?'

'For God's sake. The drama! Why did you give up acting again?' He picked up Grace, who had found an ancient Oreo and was forcing it into her mouth.

'Because I was thrown out of drama school. Remember?' Tears sprang into her eyes. 'And in case you've forgotten, they kept you on for one more year, to try and convince you you were gay.'

Grace spat the Oreo out down the front of Dan's suit. 'Bugger!' He put her down again and she began to cry. He wet the muslin and began to dab at the cloth, and then, accepting defeat, he walked into the den and shouted at the others to switch off Cartoon Network, NOW, and get into the car.

The Starbucks on Wilshire was huge. Dan sat in an armchair, the stain still visible on his left lapel, and read the *International Guardian* while Beth slumped on a sofa, eating a *biscotto*, and breastfeeding the baby, who had a scattering of crumbs over her ear. The children ran riot at the other end, climbing onto and then jumping off a horseshoe of chairs, which were luckily deserted. Occasionally Dan looked up from his paper to check that the staff weren't calling the LAPD for reinforcements, but the noise was conveniently drowned out by the sound of the cappuccino machine whirring and buzzing for the line of takeaway orders.

'Right.' It was 11.30. 'I'll be off.'

'See you back here, then.' Beth smiled wanly up at him. 'Give me a call when you're on your way.'

Dan walked twice round the block to shake all thoughts of his family off. 'Hey there! Great to meet you.' He practised his American accent. 'Fantastic day.' But when he finally came face to face with Pammy, the casting woman at CBS, he put out his hand and his greeting was as mild and British as an advert for Marmite. 'So nice to meet you.'

'And you.' She beamed. 'Come. Sit down.'

Pammy had seen his showreel and was full of praise. I really think we could use you out here,' she nodded, and she began to outline for him a new series that was coming up. 'How's your American accent?'

'Good. Pretty good.' And Dan knew if he had any guts he'd break into one right there and then. 'I was in *Streetcar*. I played Stanley Kowalski ... on the radio ...' he tailed off.

'That's just great!' Pammy beamed. 'So you're out here with your family, I hear.'

'Yes.' Dan nodded. 'My wife and ... we've got three kids. Honey, who's seven, sweet as anything but a bit of a handful, and Ben ...' Just in time he noticed her flickering eye.

'Well, I expect Finola explained this is just a general meeting. And as soon as there's something more concrete we'll have you right back in.' She paused as if remembering something. 'If only you'd been out here last month.'

'Really?'

'Well. Not to worry.' Pammy was standing up, brightening. 'We'll see you again soon.'

'Alright. Bye, then.'

'Have a great day.'

'And you. Have a ...' He coughed. 'Great day too.'

Dan stood out on the street. He took a deep breath and steadied himself, just for a minute. Maybe this is it, he thought, a lifetime of general meetings, and he imagined himself having endless great days, in his increasingly stained and filthy suit. Before calling Beth he dialled Finola's number.

'How'd it go?'

'Fine. Pretty good. She talked to me about something called *Flamingos*.'

'Oh that.' Finola sounded disappointed. 'That's not ever going to happen. But did she like you?'

'Umm. She seemed to. Yes. It was great.'

'Great!!!' Finola sounded reassured. 'Well, I'll call you as soon as there's more news.'

Dan walked slowly towards Starbucks. They could just about manage, he calculated, for three months, and then, if nothing happened, they could always fly home, and ... and stay with his mother in Epping. A car beeped and he spun round. He felt self-conscious, the only person walking, and he was sure that cars slowed a little to stare at him as they passed by. The day was warming up, the sun visible finally through the breaking clouds. 'Hey, how's it going? ' he muttered in his Stanley Kowalski, and he swore that from now on he would swim a hundred lengths and spend an hour with his language tapes working on his accent.

'How did it go?' Beth was on the pavement, overseeing running races between Ben and Honey as if they were in a 1950s slice of black-and-white film.

'Great,' he said. 'It went real swell.'

Beth glanced at him.

'I've no idea how it went. Apparently CBS can *really use me*. But the chances are I'll never hear from them again.'

Dan's phone rang in his pocket. 'Or maybe not.' It was Finola and he grinned at Beth, his spirits lifting, as he clicked it on.

'Hey, listen, Pammy's just called. Apparently you mentioned you had a real cute seven-year-old daughter. Well, they're looking for a little British girl for the lead in this new thing. It's a mixture between *Running with Wolves* and you remember that Amish film? Well, she just thought ... would Honey be available for a casting later today?'

'Let me think ...' Dan swallowed. 'Actually, Finola, I'll have to get back to you about that. OK? I'll call you back.'

'What was that about?' Beth was looking at him.

'Nothing.' Dan shook his head. 'Nothing at all.' He put his arm around her. 'Right,' he shouted to the children, who were squatting, professional as sprinters, on the pavement. 'Ready, steady, GO,' and he watched them charge towards him, their feet pounding, their arms outstretched, each wanting to be the first to grasp at the charcoal lapels of his good suit.

Crossing the River

DAVID PARK (born Belfast, 1953) has written a collection of short stories and six novels, the most recent of which are *Swallowing the Sun* (2004), and *The Truth Commissioner* (2008). The latter imagines a South African-style Truth and Reconciliation process in Northern Ireland and was awarded the Christopher Ewart-Biggs Prize. Park has also won the Authors' Club First Novel Award, the Bass Ireland Arts Award for Literature, and the University of Ulster's McCrea Literary Award. In June 2008 he was awarded the American Ireland Fund Literary Award for his contribution to Irish literature. He lives in County Down, Northern Ireland, with his wife and two children.

I TAKE THEM OVER. It's my job. As long as I can remember and probably before I can remember because here time slowly unwinds, then just when you think it's a straight line – the very way you want it to be – it coils and spools in on itself and when you try to pull an end to unravel it, everything tightens and knots. Better not to try I think, and better, too, just to concentrate on the rowing because that doesn't get any easier. My palms are long sanded smooth by the oars and fingers white-whorled with calluses – I think no one could take my fingerprints any more, even if they wanted to, but as no one has any proof that I even exist it's hardly likely they'll come calling. I have the frequent, insistent complaint of my back to tell me I do and that's good enough for me. Sometimes there is a stab of pain that makes me wince but I never let the passenger into the reason. They have passed through enough pain of their own so why would they want to hear about mine?

Sometimes I think about retirement and it's true I have enough buried coins to see me through but I've had the licence a long time and it's not something that can be given up lightly or even passed to an unenthusiastic son, who in any case has a different career in mind. And whatever anyone says about the wages there is a part of me at least that thinks of it as a calling. So I keep on rowing them across to their afterlife and every time I try to give them the best crossing that I can and of course I know how to listen and there's usually listening to be done as the bewilderment of their journey finally shakes them free from the silent shroud of death.

There are younger ones working the river now, touting for business, offering cheap price rates, but none of them has the licence and some of them would slice your throat if they thought it would get them it. But no one who has heard the stories of passengers being dumped halfway and even worse if you believe the shoreline rumours would risk stepping into their boats. I have the licence and that means the boat is sure and true, inspected once a year and hauled out of the water and subjected to the most rigorous of tests. The inspector won't renew the licence if there's any sign that it's not seaworthy and so for about three days I have to caulk and mend and scrape, give everything a brand new lining of pitch and paint. Out of the water for three days always means there's a backlog but there's no short cuts to be taken and no one gets a skimped or shoddy deal because what I understand, and what the young ones with their customised and pimped carriers all glittering with technology and toys, their sat navs and their entertainment centres, fail to grasp, is that what the customer mostly wants is reassurance – a quiet listener if they wish to speak and silence if they don't. And if I'm asked for an opinion, or get to have a choice, then I think it's probably true that the steady rhythm of the rowing and the soft caress of the oars are best for calming and carrying their souls.

I never look at the schedule. I like to take it just as it comes, stay in the moment and do what needs to be done just as it happens. So as I bring the boat alongside the jetty I have no need of name, or circumstance, and it's none of my business really and mostly it's just an unwanted distraction. In this, the first crossing of the day, my mind focuses on only the poorness of the light, the fretting choppiness of the water and the stirring, wakening swirl of the currents. He's waiting for me and as he sees my approach he looks deliberately at his watch to let me see his impatience but as I manoeuvre closer I weigh him with my eyes and gauge how low in the water the boat will sit. I offer my hand but he declines it as he steps aboard and takes his seat. His suit marks him out as a merchant and already he's brushing the weft of the cloth and running his hand through the thick rush of his hair, trying to refind the memory of who he is. I ask for the coin before the start because I know from experience that sometimes it is the wealthy who are most reluctant to pay the fare. He pats his sides and below his heart as if he's frisking himself and I see the moment of panic as he realises his pockets are empty and then finding the coin I watch him finger and turn it slowly in his hand. He's in no hurry to hand it over and he's a man who's always expected his money to work for him so I listen to him ask about an upgrade, as if there's some comfort, some hidden luxury, from which he's been excluded. I shake my head and hold out my hand for the coin but he's looking at it and weighing up the opportunities he thinks it brings. For a moment I feel a pulse of anger and want to tell him that where he's going he'll have no need of money but I know already that such words as these will only confuse and even stir him into movement that will put us both at risk, so I say nothing and merely pause and lean on the oars.

He tells me that in the other time and place he had his own boat and how much it cost and I nod as if I'm impressed. He tells me everything he owned and the list is long but after a while all I hear is the rising complaint of my back. Sometimes I think I need to caulk and oil it like the timbers of the boat. It's as if the coldness of the morning air has seeped into my spine and now nestles at the very core. My hand is still stretched towards him and he narrows his eyes and looks at the rough patina of calluses, compares it no doubt to the softness of his own fingers with their rings and their manicured nails.

'Things fell apart,' he says and his voice is thinner than before, as if it too is shaped and shivered by the cold. 'Came tumbling down like a house of cards.'

I nod as if I understand and then slowly and with a sense of pained regret he slips the coin that is completely hidden in the folds of his palm into mine, slithering it between our touching skin, as if taking the final feel of the coin to store inside the vault of his memory. I nod as if I understand and the truth is I do, because he's not the first this year and I suppose he won't be the last. And I've pieced together enough to know that on the other side the houses are tumbling, the foundations shifting in the sand and while some think it a sweet irony that those who have the most are the ones who have the most to lose, it always pains me when someone comes to me before their allotted span.

He sits back on his seat and haunches his shoulders against the cold. He has not yet had time to unlearn himself, to know that he has nothing and that now there is nothing he needs, so he asks me about names, about those who have gone before and people who were the players and shakers, about the contacts he might make, about deals that might be brokered, and I merely nod and keep the rhythm of my stroke. That's all that's true now I want to tell him but I know it's too soon for him to understand and so I let him talk and try to make his words distract from the voice in my spine that tells me my own best days are past and that one day I, too, shall make this journey for a final time.

'I had it all,' he says, gently massaging his throat as if the words have seared his flesh. 'I had it all and then it was gone. Do you understand?'

I bow my head several times and try in the gesture to show I understand and that I shall give him good service, all due respect in honour of who he was. It's an old trick but it's old because it mostly works and even now he seems to grow calmer, his hands stretching out to rest on his knees. The press of his trousers is still sharp, his leather shoes polished bright. They've let him keep his watch but I always think that a mistake. A watch in eternity – where's the point in that?

Despite his weight we're making good time and soon he's straining his eyes in the burgeoning light to see the approaching shoreline. I glance at him and see him measuring it up as the boat speeds on with a steady pull and surge, the black waters bisected by the dip and rise of the sharpened bow. It's a good rhythm and perhaps the growing light will worm its way into my spine, quieten and swaddle the complaints with warmth. But I take nothing for granted because there are currents and random eddies to be navigated and I've crossed it often enough to know that nothing can ever be taken for granted.

'There's no shoreline development,' he says, his eyes narrowing into slits as he scans the distance. 'Wasted opportunity,' he says. 'Whatever the market, people always like to look out over water. It's a sure-fire thing. Copper-bottomed. Can't go wrong.' And when he asks me what I think I nod again and puff a little stream of air through the purse of my lips to show that I need all my strength and concentration to bring him safely ashore.

We're almost there now and he's getting more excited. He's talking about deals, about opportunities, and he's offering me a chance of a guaranteed return on my investment which will see me in a comfortable retirement without the need to work another day. As I moor at the jetty he tells me he'll give me his card and I watch as he pats his pockets once more and then he burrows his hand into his inside breast pocket and when he pulls it out empty he stares at that emptiness before slumping back on his seat. Then he furrows a hand through his hair again and loosens his tie before opening his collar and that's when I glimpse the red scar of the rope and I turn my eyes away because it's not something I want him to see I've seen. So after we dock he slowly rises to his feet and this time he takes my help-ing hand as he steps ashore and for a second I think he's rummaging in his back pocket for a tip, a tip that under the terms of the licence I wouldn't be able to accept, but he pats me twice on the shoulder as a thank you and then he's gone. And for a second I sit listening to the sound of his leather-soled shoes on the wooden planks of the jetty and then as they slowly fade into silence I push off again and pull once more on the oars.

You get days like this when everything is tricky and the passengers present more problems than the currents. There's those whose lives have been taken from them and whose anger sometimes rocks the boat, who've had no time to prepare, and I have to watch them finger their wounds as they do a kind of autopsy on themselves, confused by the sudden flowering of their own blood-blossomed bodies, des-perate even to deny their ownership as if there's been a mix-up and they've been issued with someone else's. Children, too, can bring their own problems, more than could ever be described – not least those who think they've stumbled through some cavernous wardrobe and are heading towards an adventure where they will ride on the back of a lion. You have to tell them again and again to sit down, that they can't help with the rowing, that this river offers no chance of dolphin or whale sightings. And of course there are the frightened, those who want their mothers (but strangely rarely their fathers), and sometimes I have to talk them all the way across, tell them stories or even, although I've no longer the voice for it, sing some of the old songs I remember from the childhood I must once have had.

So now as she gets in the boat I feel only a sense of relief. These rarely give any trouble. They've been travelling such a long time that one more crossing means little to them. She scrunches up on the plain wooden bench that passes for a seat as if leaving room for others to join her and when I tell her there's no need, that she's the only passenger, she brings her hands together as if she's praying and smiles. She's dressed in black and her hair, too, is black as the water and tied in a ponytail that sometimes the wind stirs a little and curls into a question mark but from experience I know she will ask little of me, that despite everything that's happened to her she will do nothing but trust. It's always been all she's ever had to cling to even though she knows by now that there is no truth in trust. So I'll do my best for her, do my best to be true, take her only where she needs to go. And before I can even ask she's taking out the coin that she's hidden in her clothing and unfolding the silk handkerchief in which it's wrapped. I wonder how many other coins she's had to pay to those who promised to take her to where she wanted to go and how many of them lied.

Already she will have crossed water, perhaps many times, starting even in a boat not much bigger than this and then who knows in what lurching, rolling holds of ships, the captive air hot and fetid? Or in the backs of lorries for many days, pushed in tight with others who share no names but only the embarrassment of their bodies and who are forbidden to speak. I glance at her and know she's so used to silence that it's what's most comfortable for her and it's only the occasional flick of her eyes over her shoulder that says she's still worried about what may be following her. I want to tell her she's safe now, for a second ask her to tell me her story, but it's against the rules so it's only the oars I let whisper in their little flurries and frets of white.

She's not very old, young enough to be someone's daughter, old enough to be someone's wife, and somewhere there will be people who wonder where she is and when she's coming back. Her face is open, curiously smooth and unbruised by death and her eyes are brown but strangely glittering and shiny as if freshly washed by rain. Her hands hold the edges of the seat as if she thinks we might hit a sudden wave that will throw her into the depths. I want to tell her that I know the currents, that I've never yet lost a passenger, that she's safe with me, but I know she'd only smile and that her eyes would still be edged with fear. She looks out at the water and as the boat lifts a little in the swell I see her knuckles blanch as her hands tighten their grip. And then I understand – it's been a while since I've sat facing such a one so I've forgotten the signs. I tell her it won't be much longer, that I'll soon have her ashore, and she smiles quickly and bows her head submissively. It makes me want to tell her that I am her servant, not she mine, that I know how frightened she is of the water, but because she doesn't understand that we are destined to die only once I pull a little stronger, ignoring the fresh complaint of my back.

'Will I be able to get in touch with my family, tell them that I'm here?' she suddenly asks. Her voice is fluttering, light-winged.

'In time they'll know where you are and in time all of them will be able to come here too,' I answer, avoiding the bright glitter of her eyes.

'Will you bring them across?' she asks.

'I'll bring them all.'

'But I have no more money to pay you.' And then she begins to cry and I know her tears are salted with the sea and even when I tell her that there is no need to worry she continues and then she looks at me and asks if there is some other way she can pay. But before I can answer she tells me how long it is since she saw her family, that they will be worried about her, that she has a younger sister and she's frightened that she too will be deceived by the promises, then sold. How she will do anything to prevent that happening.

I swear to her that I shall bring them all, that I shall row each one safely to where she is and that I want nothing more from her than to do good service, to bring her to where will be her home, and I tell her it's a place where she will never have to pay someone or be used by a man again. She lifts her face to me and I do not know whether she is able to believe my words or not. I want to tell her that all I traffic in is souls and for a strange moment I wish that I was her father and could look after her until she knows the words are true. It's breaking the codes of practice, of course, to think things like that, but the mind is a strange thing and not always given to sticking to the letter of the law. I must be getting old because as the skin on my palms hardens I fear that something's softening inside and I know that's no use in a job like this – perhaps another sign after all that it's time to hang up the oars, sell the licence to someone younger.

We're almost there now and she falls calm and still. She knows that this will be her new home but probably sees it as temporary, a stopover until she finds where it is she really wants to go. They scatter across the world like so much ash blown on the wind and I do not know if they ever find the place they're looking for or if it exists only in their heads. I raise the oars and let our motion drift us closer to the jetty and now her face is marked by relief. She bows her head in gratitude and then I help her out of the boat and she feels so light that I think death has made her weightless, that all the encumbrances life burdened her with have finally fallen away. For a few moments she stands watching as I pull away again and then she turns and disappears into the veiled distance.

It's a busy day and there is no time for rest except the two official breaks that health and safety regulations insist I take. Moored on the shore I take some bread and a little wine but measured out and not enough to push me over the limit. And then it's more crossings and here is a soldier, straight-backed in his uniform, his medal glinting in the light, and in the fix of his gaze I, too, try to straighten and find some show of discipline in my rowing. He has no fear that he will let himself parade for the likes of me and no words cross his lips and perhaps he looks at this as one more posting to some far-off land where there is a job to do. I'm curious about the medal and wonder if it's one of those that are given for being there or is it for some special act of bravery. He's still being brave and his eyes hold the distance unwaveringly and for a second I want to tell him that the war, that all wars, are over for him now. But I row on because it's not my place to tell him these things or that soon he will meet the one he last saw in the sights of his weapon.

There are others this day who call themselves soldiers but are now only the young boys they always were and they're shivering in their sports gear, their hooded heads dropped towards their chests, their skittering eyes trying to understand their badge of honour, the neat little medal that gains them admittance to a world that lies beyond the only boundaries they once knew and thought they were defending. One calls me 'Old Man' and asks me what I'm looking at but in most of them their bravado has been burnt away by death and the shock of their own blood slowly haloing them on city pavements wet with rain, the memory of the terrible chasm of silence that opened up when the life support machine was turned off, and as we approach the opposite shore they ply me with questions about turf ownership and neighbourhoods. But all I know is that when they die they die alone and it doesn't matter what the posted messages say – those text-spelt tributes in cyberspace about true soldiers. This now is their journey across the river and they're making it before their allotted span and when they shiver it's not just because of the coldness and so I take these, too, with respect and with all due care.

The day is almost over now and the fading light rather than the schedule tells me that I have one final journey to make before my back gets the rest it's started to demand. I approach the shore for this last passenger and narrowing my eyes I can see that she's small, white-haired, fragile in frame, trembling like the final leaf on a winter tree. When she sees me she holds up her hand as if she's hailing me. I raise my arm to let her know I've seen her, then grip the oars tightly and try to steady myself. It's the one I knew was coming and which I sought in vain to be excused. 'No exceptions,' was what they said when I begged to be released. 'You know the rules.'

She needs to be helped into the boat and I put a blanket over her shoulders to try and stem the cold. Her eyes are fogged and webbed with death and she sits in the boat just as straight-backed as she sits in the chair in the small room they've allocated her, the place where I go to visit her while the plaques and the tangles spread and smother the light. But whatever the names the scientists give, I think of it as a thief, each day robbing something more of who she is and by now there's only fleeting glimpses left, revealed in a little joke perhaps because that capacity while worn thin is still allowed to her, or a phrase that suddenly sparks out of the cold ash of memory.

And after I've gone she will forget that I've been but they say I should be grateful that she still knows who I am. Now as I look into her eyes for that same recognition they are clouded and veiled by the bewilderment of death. I row more gently than I have ever rowed before, trying to steady the beat of my heart by synchronising it with my pull on the oars. There are so many things that I should say but don't know how, and if I were to say them perhaps their finality would upset, so I hug them close and tell myself that perhaps in time I shall find words that will be worthy enough to carry her into an afterlife. So now I just row and keep on trying to row as softly and gently as I know how.

'Don't you need a rest? she asks after a while and she rubs her eyes as if she's been sleeping and is beginning to wake.

'No, I'm fine,' I say. 'It's my job to take you across. And it's not long now. Not long to go now.'

'You're doing a good job,' she says. But before I can answer she hesitates then asks, 'Is that you?'

'Yes, it's me.'

'I thought it was but I wasn't sure. I didn't know it was you taking me. Are you sure you know the way?'

'Yes and I'll not lose you.'

'Will I be going home soon?' she asks and looks closely at my face as she always does when she asks this, as if she wants to gauge if I'm going to tell her the truth.

'You're going home soon.'

'That's good,' she says. 'I can't remember what the house looks like any more. I think in the street there's hardly any of the old neighbours left.'

'Just the Boyles and the Fallows – that's all who's left now,' I tell her.

'Just the Boyles and the Fallows, and George next door – that's right,' she says as if she's confirming something important to herself. 'I'm tired now. When you're going home will you turn off the lights and make sure all the plugs are out?'

'Yes, I'll check everything. Don't worry.'

There is a moment of silence before she asks again, 'Will I be going home soon?' asking again because already she's forgotten the answer to her question.

Yes, you're finally going home. You're going across the river and when you get there Bobby will be waiting and all your sisters who came before you. All of them waiting for you.

We're almost there. The last vestiges of light are draining from the sky and it's hard now to see where water and horizon meet. I feel the coldness flooding my bones as I glance behind me to take my final bearings and then when I turn again she's holding her outstretched hand to me with a coin in it.

'You forgot to take the money,' she says. 'You'll never be a businessman.'

'I can't take it,' I say.

'Don't be silly,' she tells me. 'What do I need it for?'

'I can't,' I say again, shaking my head.

'Then give it to the children.'

I have to look away, look into the distance where the water is inky black and spirals into the unknown mysteries of the currents. How can I take the coin? How can I take the coin when everything has been already paid in full?

'Take it,' she says and her voice is gentle but insistent so I hold out my hand on this last journey and take the coin I never wanted to be given, then bow my head and carry her across the river, my oars slowly rising and falling in one final, silent salutation of a son's love.

Kaltes klares
Wasser

HARI KUNZRU was born in 1969 and lives in London and New York. His first novel, *The Impressionist*, was the winner of the Betty Trask Prize 2002 and led to his inclusion as one of Granta's Best of Young British Novelists in 2003. His second novel, *Transmission*, won him the inaugural 'decibel' award at the British Book Awards and was named a *New York Times* notable book of the year. In 2005 he published *Noise*, a short story collection. His latest novel is *My Revolutions* (2007).

I'VE GIVEN THEM ALL NICKNAMES. The Minister, the woman from the Foundation, the sleek new rep from the pharmaceutical company. Stupid nicknames that come of their own accord, spawned out of the marshy recesses of my brain, the indefinable area I associate with swelling and bad dreams.

The minister has always been Futureshock, ever since our first long meeting several years ago. Walking into the room with his entourage he did all he could to appear imposing, institutional, but mainly he looked astonished, his bug eyes and slightly slack mouth giving him the expression of a cartoon character who's just spotted a truck bearing down on him. Unfortunate, I thought at first. Forty minutes into the session, as it became clear his understanding of the disease was (let's put it diplomatically) *broad-brush*, I realised his goggle-face was the expression of an existential state. Shock and awe. The man was looking into tomorrow and knew he couldn't do a thing about it: all the shit he was supposed to be dealing with was going to break over him like a tsunami over a package tourist.

Is it me, that nicknaming part of my consciousness? Or a sequela, a residue of my last bout of fever? That, if you didn't notice, is a deep question. Do my thoughts belong to me, doc, or the parasites in my blood? Last year was the third time I've been sick and by far the worst. To coin a phrase, I haven't been myself since. I try to stay on track, but things tend to slide. So, me or my shot-away neurology? Show of hands please.

The minister runs a finger inside the collar of his neatly tailored safari suit and explains that the big problem is the people don't exist. The people don't exist because their villages don't exist, because the land on which their villages stand is still officially forest, and forest, by definition, can only contain officially recognised forest villages, which these aren't. The government wants more forest, not less. It has ecological targets to meet. So the people aren't going to exist any time soon and if they don't exist, they can't be helped, because what government has an obligation to the non-existent?

Enola Gay, the Foundation representative, nods at this, as if it isn't completely insane. Enola has that moneyed East Coast trick of suppressing her sweat glands, so that even though the aircon in this conference room isn't working and the temperature is in the high thirties, she looks clean and bright and new in her Egyptian cottons and little pearl earrings. Maybe she's coated in something. Is there a kind of sealant spray you can buy?

When I got sick last time I went blind. It's supposed to be poetic, the dying of the light. To me it was just scary. The blindness was preceded by a strange dissociative strobing, as if I was way back behind myself, then in myself again for a while, then back, then in, on and on, each phase lasting – I don't know. I had no sense of time. I'd been thinking about conducting a seance, or dreaming I was actually doing so, though in my dream there was none of that old-fashioned spiritualist paraphernalia, no flickering candles or Ouija boards. It was a kind of diving down. I somehow dived down and found myself in the land of the dead. When I came up again I was blind.

We have an uninvited guest on the biscuit plate. Fat little *anopheles*, squatting on the rim like a tiny spy, the enemy's eyes and ears at our bi-monthly council of war. Because the rest of us, all of us round this Formica-topped plywood table, are on the same side. That's important to keep in your head at those moments when you feel like taking the invisible rail-gun out of your invisible sports bag full of weaponry and blasting the hell out of the whole lot of them while screaming in cathartic wordless anguish.

Being blind, it was as if part of death had come back with me. As if death was a smoked-glass lens through which (*henceforth, evermore*) I would be forced to view the world. And my sight didn't just come back. As in: *the next morning I woke up and I felt better and I could see again*. It was a battle. It was metaphysical. I had to fight the forces of blindness and vanquish them.

The biscuits have been laid out in a fan array, those sickly sweet biscuits that are the only brand you can get here and taste like all the bad snack foods of the world concentrated into individual crumbly yellow-white rectangles. I've eaten two so far. I watch as the mosquito makes a brief flight and settles right in the middle of the formal arrangement. *Lord of all I survey. Soon the world shall know my name.* It shows pride in your work, that array. A tea-boy on the way up.

Her hair looks like someone ironed it. Enola with the jellyfish eyes, are you actually human? We had a personal conversation once, on her last visit. I was drunk (no surprise there) and confessional, and started talking about all the things I shouldn't, about meaning and purpose and absurdity and how I worry about falling off the edge of the world because of the weeks that go by when I don't talk to anyone about anything that isn't work, and mostly I don't talk to anyone at all. She adopted a wooden expression of concern she'd obviously learnt on a course and uttered a series of clichés so devastating in their banality, their utter lack of acknowledgement of my particular human existence, that I started to laugh and kept on laughing until she got up and said she had to be getting back to her suite because she had email to write. She actually used the phrase 'getting back to my suite'. Oh yes, that vital high-status reception room. How I howled. I admit I'd hoped she was going to sleep with me, but that was in the early part of the evening, before I realised her idea of sex probably involved beaming something to you from her PDA.

Who is there to tell, anyway? Who could do anything?

The Minister has got onto the subject of drugs, the cheap ones which don't work any more and the expensive ones which do. Poor Futureshock. You only get so much money to play with and coming in under budget earns you your choice of: a) one-on-one tea with the president, b) a new limo, or c) a statue (three-quarter bust or even full length) in a rural development area. So who says the cheap drugs don't work? Officially they still do, because Futureshock hasn't approved a study, and until he approves that study and it shows to his satisfaction that the cheap drugs don't work, the official position will remain that they do, that all the millions of doses of under-budget but useless medicine he sends out to the rural areas are actually curing people.

You know, Enola, I've changed my mind. I think sex with you might be good, in a rubber-dolly kind of a way. You're what? Thirty-five? Mayflower stock. Good cheekbones, expensive prep schools, MBA, health-club membership. You're in personal control of twenty million dollars of media-baron guilt money. You'd go one way or the other. You might snap, let it all out, want to do a lot of nasty stuff you'd have to run away from on the treadmill the next morning. Or you might just go AWOL: lie back, assume the textbook positions. Spreadsheets, spread between the sheets. Enola enters strategic alliance then puts the incline on max.

Q. What does the Land of the Dead look like?

A. It's dark but not black. It's a differentiated field of grey and the dead are part of that grey, waves inflecting its flow. The dead are vibrations, undulations. When you pass through them, for a brief moment they inhabit you.

I ground my teeth. I fought the blindness, forcing it outwards, tunnelling through it, all the time experiencing a warping of self, a pulse and stretch that threw me out to the horizon of things, then sucked me back inside the cramped knot of my jaw until my consciousness achieved infinite density, became a pinpoint of high white pain. It came to me that this cosmic proprioceptive rhythm had a purpose and if only I surrendered to it I could do unprecedented things, flow through all the parasites in all the mosquitoes and suck them back into my head, draw them into myself until I'd cleansed every far-flung marsh and puddle of the world. I would heal everyone. Me. I could already feel *p. falciparum* building up in drifts in the deep recesses of my brain, clogging my arteries with infected red cells. My swollen head expanded, vast with fever.

Back in meeting-space we're onto IP law, courtesy of Face-off. The thing about Face-off is he's doing us a favour by even being here and we shouldn't upset him. He's currently inhabiting the body of a lightly bronzed German in his early fifties, a conspicuously well-dressed cycling or skiing type who was introduced to me as Kirch or Koch or Kirchner, something like that. The name of the host body is unimportant, because we all know it's Face-off and he always needs to be smiled at and coaxed and propitiated like a primitive idol, even by Enola Gay if she wants more bang for her Foundation buck. This Koch, with his penny loafers and emphatic consonants, is gently threatening Futureshock concerning a local company who are making a generic version of one of his products. Not for malaria. God forbid! Malaria isn't what you'd call a revenue-rich ailment. This factory is making an exact copy of his fancy heart disease medicine and selling it for about a tenth of the branded price. Unlike low-disposable-income developing-world villagers, Westerners have lifestyle preferences and one of their key lifestyle preferences is to be alive instead of dead. They pay good money for it, unless of course they don't have to. Koch/Face-off is legally required to maximise shareholder value. Legally required, you understand. That means aggressively protecting the company's intellectual property: it would be negligent to do anything else. Koch performs his routine well, delivers the well-worn lines with considerable aplomb. We're asked to imagine the personal consequences for him if he gave way to his highly developed sentiments, the lawsuits, the damages he would face if he allowed his natural thirst for justice and keen empathy for the suffering of others to colour his professional judgement. A slippery slope. A morality tale: Losing the summer house; tearfully kissing little Gudrun or Ulrike goodbye. The cops making a point of keeping the cuffs on for the cameras on the court-house steps.

If Futureshock opens his mouth any wider, he'll start to dribble. What should we do if baby turns blue?

I remember drinking once with a guy called Prosper, a saturnine Ivoirian lab tech from one of our projects in the south. We were in their team house, which wasn't bad as team houses go. Intermittent electricity supply, functioning shower. For four days we'd been unable to go out to the clinic because of a rebel attack on the main road out of town. I was beginning to go a little crazy. I'd already had a meaningless row with the team leader because I lit a cigarette in the communal area. I was a visitor, I was under her authority. That's how it works, but they lose perspective out there, get that Alamo mentality and start to believe the metaphorical hordes will pour over the wall if there's the slightest infraction of discipline. I mean, it's not like I needed a lecture on public health. I suppose I shouldn't have said what I said, but fuck it. It was only a cigarette. So there was a *huis clos* atmosphere over dinner and everyone went to bed early, except Prosper, who sat in a chair on the verandah listening to trebly hymns on his personal stereo. I was bored and angry and I'd already mined the others for conversation. My days of forced inactivity were making me feel like a Beirut hostage: I might as well have been chained to a radiator.

My secret weapon was the bottle of locally distilled rum I'd brought from the capital. It tasted like industrial cleaner, gave you the shits along with your hangover and had the sole virtue of flensing the insides in such a way as to lend the drinker a temporary (and spurious) sense of being scoured, emptied of whatever physical or psychic filth had driven you to open it in the first place. I offered Prosper a glass, waving it in his field of vision until he took off the headphones. To my surprise he accepted.

We drank and talked, or rather we drank and Prosper grudgingly answered my questions about his family, his home, when he first volunteered. His responses weren't particularly illuminating. Did he like being a lab technician? Very much. Would he volunteer for another tour? Of course. Why of course? Because he was needed. Once or twice (out of politeness, as far as I could tell) he asked similar questions of me. But he drank, which was the main thing. He drank and listened as I babbled about whatever came into my head, constructing both sides of the conversation I so badly craved. After a while the rum began to work and I no longer cared whether he was interested. I told him about growing up in Leeds, going to medical school in the early eighties. How I pierced my ear, bleached my hair white. Not many post-punk medical students, Prosper. Did he know about punk and new wave? He nodded without conviction and held out his glass. I refilled it, went on. Darkness was cool. Black clothes. I spent all my money on records, used the names of the bands as a kind of shorthand for a mental state, a sort of epic depression. The point wasn't to get happy, merely to raise up your unhappiness, make it bearable.

I was wittering on, trying to describe this ridiculous subculture to a man who'd grown up in a place defined by the mission school, the army checkpoint and the fields. Had Prosper ever bought a record? Tapes, he said. Cassette tapes. His eyes were glassy. I told him how there was even a band. An all-girl German band, very underground. Prosper shook his head. *Malaria*. Why would anyone want to have such a name?

Enola is making an actuarial point to the Minister, something about per-dollar mortality reduction. Well, well. I heard a rumour they were in partnership. Looks like it's true. Enola is saying that for each dollar spent she wants to save as many lives or fractions of lives (her expression) as she can. Face-off is charitably offering a discount on his antimalarial drugs, and if the deal works out she'll effectively save twice as many people. No brainer, right?

An arrangement. Complex, private, opaque and yet no doubt rigorously contractual. The Foundation lends its good name, and—

The problem is, says Enola. Here it comes. If the Foundation is to attract a private partner in its efforts to save the lives of the Minister's citizens, it's important such a partner feels comfortable about the stability of the local regulatory environment.

What was their song? The Malaria song?

Kaltes klares Wasser
Über meinen Körper

I was trying to remember the song for Prosper. *Cold clear water*. But I couldn't make the phrase come into my mind. I don't know why I began to cry. Because my body was fucked; because I had no more resources to call on. Prosper put an arm round my shoulders. What you need, he said, is Jesus in your life.

I'm so tired. A four-hour journey over lunar dirt roads, a plane and three more hours of hydrocarbon-laced gridlock to get here. Across the table Futureshock looks grim. He's not really listening, still stuck on the fact that, even with a discount, Face-off's new drugs are still more expensive than the old ones. If he budges at all, he'll fail to meet his target. He won't get the three-piece suite or the rotisserie set and the opposition will accuse him of not caring about the health of the poor, which he doesn't particularly, though that's not the point.

They're gradually revealing the shape of the proposition. Want a free malaria programme? Shut down the generics factory. I'd say the chances of Futureshock buying it are slim. The factory's probably owned by his cousin, whereas the people out in the south are refugees, only visible at all in an administrative sense because irritating foreigners keep harping on about them. The Minister has better things to do with his time – discrediting the opposition in the press, renumbering his offshore accounts. Far better to shelve this. Better for me, too. My head is spinning. The prophet Ezekiel's vision: wheels within wheels. Was that some kind of desert fever? Could it have been treated? I no longer have my ethical bearings. I don't feel well. Just let me go home to bed; I don't know left from right any more, let alone right from wrong. That must be a song lyric. But what song?

A fever like I had doesn't pass by without leaving marks. I was incredibly gaunt, wore dark glasses indoors. I'd turned into *The Man Who Fell to Earth*. There were months of headaches, holding onto the banisters as I climbed the stairs. It was the longest time I'd been back in England in twelve years. Children had mobile phones. The radio was dominated by a ruthless repetitive thumping. When I looked into the mirror I saw an old man with sagging pouches under his eyes and a yellow cast to his skin. As soon as I got stronger I flew back out here. I'm based in the capital. A co-ordinating role: I'm not up to spending months at a time in the field. And my old face has never returned. The parasites scored deep lines across my forehead, turned down the corners of my mouth.

So Enola, I don't blame you for not wanting to go to bed with me. What am I offering? I'm a borderline alcoholic whose shattered body lets him down in inventive and humiliating ways and whose main emotional reference points are early-eighties records. My one meaningful attachment was a two-year student affair with a woman whose only noticeable effect on my life was to accelerate my flight. For twenty years I've worked in far-flung corners of the earth where my total inability to commit to another human being can be disguised as a generalised passion for humanity. The poor bastards huddle in line and I love them, from a distance.

The mosquito has vanished from the biscuit plate. In a moment, someone round the table will reach up a hand, slap an exposed arm, the nape of their neck. Who will it be? I'm supposed to speak next, to outline our position, make a case. What will come out of my mouth? I could have done with a day to sleep before this meeting. Or a month. I think I could actually manage it, if I had a catheter. And perhaps some kind of drip. A month of unconsciousness. Cold water over my arms, my face. What will I say? Love me, Enola. Evolution is ahead of us anyway. There's no time. The room has gone silent. They're waiting for me to speak.

What She Did on Her
Summer Vacation

ZOË HELLER was born in London in 1965. She is the author of three novels: *Everything You Know* (1999), *Notes on a Scandal* (2003), which was Booker shortlisted and made into a feature film starring Cate Blanchett and Judi Dench, and *The Believers* (2008). She lives in New York.

SAND FLIES ARE DANCING in the glare of Cheyenne's head-lamp as she pants along the beach at dusk. Pfoot, pfoot, haaa. Her legs are flecked with seaweed and breaded with sand. Her hair is hanging in wet strands against her cheek. In her arms, she is juggling the liquid heft of a large, sea-sodden dog.

When she glimpses a pale figure moving about at the foot of the sand dunes, she halts. 'Hello?' she calls out. 'Excuse me?'

The spectral shape is silent. She walks forward, calling again. 'Hello!'

Out of the gloom, a man appears: tall, red-haired, wearing khaki pants and flip-flops. He is standing on the bottom step of a wooden staircase that leads to one of the beachfront houses.

'Hi – sorry – can you help me?' Cheyenne asks.

The man raises a hand to shade his eyes from her head-lamp. 'I don't know,' he says, in a drawling, English accent. 'What do you want help with?'

'I found this dog by the rocks,' she says. 'He's breathing funny and he can't stand up.'

'Oh dear. Poor doggy-wog.'

Doggy-wog? She squints at him. 'He doesn't have a collar. I don't know what to do with him.'

'May I ask how old you are?'

'Sorry?'

'I said—'

'I'm fourteen.'

'I only ask because it seems rather late for a young girl to be out on the beach alone.'

Cheyenne sucks in her cheeks. 'Actually, the manager at my hotel said it was totally safe for me to run in the evenings.'

'Oh, did he?'

'Yeah. He's lived on the island for seven years and he's never heard of anyone being attacked on this beach.'

The man looks away, bored with the subject now. 'He's probably been poisoned,' he says, nodding at the dog.

'Really?' Cheyenne's eyes widen. 'How can you tell?'

'I'm just guessing. They do a lot of dog-poisoning around here.'

'Oh my God, that's horrible.'

'The natives aren't terribly keen on dogs.'

'So, what do you think I should do with him?'

He shrugs. 'I haven't a clue.'

Cheyenne stares. She is not accustomed to having adults take her crises lightly. 'Well, do you have a phone that I could use to call someone?'

'Who were you thinking of calling, exactly?'

'I don't know – like, a vet?'

A shadow of a smile passes across the man's face. 'No vets on this island, I'm afraid.'

'How do you know?'

'Because *I've* been on this island for ten years.'

Cheyenne thinks about this. 'Is there a doctor?'

'There is, yes – a rather sweet Ghanaian man – but he'll have closed the clinic by now. And I doubt, in any case, that he'd be interested in treating a dog.'

'What am I supposed to do, then? I can't just leave him.'

'I think you'll have to.'

A sob enters Cheyenne's voice. 'But he's really sick! And I've carried him almost a mile already. I'm sorry, but I'm not going to walk away and let him die.'

'All right,' the man says. 'Calm down.' He stares at her irritably, then turns and begins walking up the steps. 'Come.'

'Are you taking me to your house?' she asks.

'No, to my torture chamber. It's where I keep all the naughty little girls I find on the beach.'

She stands silently debating with herself for a moment. Then, she hitches up the slippery dog in her arms and staggers after him. He does not offer to carry the dog.

'What's your name?' she enquires, as they climb the stairs.

He glances back sharply, as if she had asked something impertinent. 'Hugh. What's yours?'

'Cheyenne-Louise Harris.'

'What an extraordinary name.'

'My mom had a pet bird called Cheyenne when she was little and she always—'

'Where are you staying?'

She pauses, allowing the rudeness of his interruption to resonate. 'At the Frangipani.'

'Of course you are. Like it there, do you?'

'It's okay,' she says, warily. 'The pool's nice.'

'Ri-ight. What is it these days – some sort of "infinity" thing with waterfalls and gold dolphins?'

'No … it's just really big.'

At the top of the stairs, they pass through a gate and come out on the deck of a white clapboard house. Several chaise longues are arranged around its edges, and at the centre, a long trestle table has been set for a dinner party.

'Wait here,' Hugh says. He opens some curtained French windows and steps inside the house. There is just time to hear him say, 'We have a visitor,' before the door closes.

Cheyenne stands on the deck, studying the peeling Hello Kitty stickers on her sneakers. The only things she has eaten today are a tangerine and an *Oh Henry!* bar. Her stomach is beginning to growl. Presently, she walks over to one of the chaise longues and lays the dog down. She is just taking off her headlamp, when Hugh re-emerges, holding a cell phone.

He is followed by a tall, fair-haired woman, wearing a blue silk kaftan and lots of tinkling, gold bangles. She glances at Cheyenne and then at the dog and puts her head back inside the French windows. 'Clarice?' she calls. 'Would you bring down two beach towels please?'

'This is my wife, Caroline,' Hugh says. 'Caroline, this is Cheyenne.'

Caroline smiles with closed eyes as she shakes Cheyenne's hand. 'Nice to meet you.'

'Hi-ee,' Cheyenne sing-songs.

The man hands her the phone. 'Here you go. The doctor's number is 7006. You dial 323 first.'

While Cheyenne tentatively taps out the number, Caroline goes over to the table and examines the place settings. 'Darling, are you sure we want to put Lysette next to Francis?'

'Please don't ask me to do the placement,' her husband says, 'if you're going to second-guess my decisions.'

Caroline laughs, as if his unpleasantness were a wonderful joke.

'By the way,' he adds, 'are you aware that your dress is completely transparent?'

'Is it?' She smiles down at herself.

'I'm always delighted to see your snatch, but I think we might want to spare our guests the anatomy lesson, don't you?'

Cheyenne stares pinkly at the floor, pretending to be intent on her phone call.

An elderly black woman comes out onto the deck now, carrying two towels. Caroline points at the chaise longue. 'Could you put those under the dog, Clarry?'

Grunting with effort, the woman lays out the towels and heaves the dog onto them.

'No one's answering,' Cheyenne says, holding the phone away from her ear. 'Is there anyone else we could call?'

Hugh shakes his head. 'That's it, I'm afraid.'

'Are you sure?'

'Why don't we call that woman who lives down the Narrows?' Caroline suggests.

Hugh frowns. 'I haven't the faintest clue who you're talking about.'

'Yes you do! The woman who rounds up the cats and takes them to Nassau to be spayed. With the yellow hair ...

Estella! She might have an idea what to do. Do we have her number, darling?'

'Why on earth would we have her number?'

'Who would, I wonder?'

'I must say, I think this is all getting a little preposterous.'

'I bet Duncan has it.'

'You bloody phone him, then.'

Cheyenne, noticing that the dog is stirring, kneels down to pet him. 'Hi sweetie,' she murmurs, 'how are you doing?' She wonders whether Caroline is watching her, and if so, whether she is touched by her affection for the animal. When she looks up, Caroline is facing the other way, talking into the phone.

'Duncan! It's me, Caro. God, can you hear me? You sound as if you're in China ... No, no, dinner's still on. I'm just calling for Estella's number. *Estella*, the woman who – no, you silly goose, of course not. We've got a girl here ... it's too complicated to go into now. Could you just give me the number? Thank you, darling.'

The dog is making a wobbly attempt at standing up.

'Oh goody, he's better,' Hugh says. 'Can we take him back to the beach now?' He leans down and addresses himself to the animal. 'I'm right, aren't I, Bonzo? You'd like to go back to the beach, wouldn't you?'

The dog cants his head in Hugh's direction. He opens his mouth slowly, as if to yawn, and then throws up.

'Fucking Christ!' Hugh shouts, as black, foul-smelling vomit gushes over the chaise and onto the deck.

'Sorry, Duncan,' Caroline says brightly, 'I'm going to have to call you back.'

The three of them stand in silence for a moment, looking at the spreading black puddle on the floor. Cheyenne is about to offer to fetch paper towels, when the dog utters a long, low moan and collapses back onto the towels, dead.

'You must never do something like that again, okay?' Mr Harris tells his daughter later that night, over dinner at the Frangipani's Pink Bar restaurant. 'I know you meant well, but that dog could have had diseases. It could have had rabies.'

Cheyenne's adventure with the dog has introduced a bracing element of peril into the becalmed world of the Harris family vacation. She has been back an hour and already the story is beginning to take on the classical dimensions of myth.

'Your dad's right, Shy,' Mrs Harris says. 'I don't want you going on the beach after dark any more.' She smiles at a waitress, who is waiting to pour rum punch into her glass. 'Just a little bit, thank you, dear.'

Friday night is barbecue night at the Pink Bar. Outside on the terrace, men in toques are grimacing over smoky grills and women in brightly coloured aprons are doling ice-cream scoops of potato salad onto paper plates. Inside, not far from where Cheyenne and her parents are sitting, a local band is playing 'Please Mr Postman' on steel drums.

'Even in the daytime,' Mr Harris says, 'you shouldn't be walking into strangers' houses. It isn't safe.'

Cheyenne, who is rather enjoying the fuss, rolls her eyes. 'It was an emergency, Dad.'

'It doesn't matter. Those people could have been anybody. You don't know what kind of weirdos are out there.'

'They *were* kind of weird, as it happens,' she says, provocatively.

Mrs Harris leans forward. 'Weird, how? I thought they were nice to you.'

'They were. They were just very ... you know, English. They kept saying these really rude and inappropriate things to each other.'

Her mother and father exchange glances. 'They didn't say anything inappropriate to you, did they?' her mother asks.

'No, no. They were super-nice.'

'How old were they?'

'I don't know.'

'Well, were they older, younger?'

'Pretty old.'

'Like our age?'

Cheyenne considers her mother briefly. Mrs Harris has had a massage earlier in the evening and her wrinkled forehead is still slick with massage oil. 'No, they were definitely younger than you guys.'

'Was the woman attractive?'

'Oh my God, yes. Gorgeous. Her skin was, like, flawless.'

'And did the man mention anything about what he did for a living?' Mr Harris asks.

'Uh-uh.'

Mr Harris nods thoughtfully. 'I'd imagine they are privately wealthy.'

'Was their house nice?' Mrs Harris asks.

'Oh yeah.'

'How was it furnished?'

Cheyenne pauses. In the excitement of relating her story, she has perhaps slightly exaggerated the extent of her dealings with the English couple. 'I didn't really see inside,' she confesses. 'I was mostly out on the deck.'

'They didn't invite you in?'

'Well, I wanted to stay with the dog.'

'But they were friendly to you, right?'

'Yes, Mom.'

Another waitress approaches now, carrying a wicker basket filled with bread rolls.

'Thank you, sweetie,' Mr Harris says, picking out two rolls with the specially provided tongs.

Mrs Harris wags her finger jokingly. 'Take that away! Don't you be tempting me.' She steals a sideways glance at Cheyenne's plate. 'You're not eating your salad, Shy.'

Cheyenne makes a face. 'It tastes weird. Like it's got chlorine on it.'

'They have to wash it in disinfectant to make sure there's no bacteria on it,' her mother says.

'Why didn't you say you didn't like it?' her father demands. 'Go get something else.'

'No, it's okay.'

'I'm paying fifty dollars a head for this buffet. If it's no good, you should have something else.'

'Fine.' Cheyenne grabs wolfishly at one of her father's rolls and begins to butter it. 'I'll have this.'

'Oh look! It's Kevin and Laura!' Mrs Harris cries, pointing to a mousy-looking man and woman who have just entered the restaurant. She beckons them over. Kevin and Laura are honeymooners from Chicago. They are not an attractive couple. Laura has lank hair and bad posture. Kevin wears creepy sandals and old-man slacks. But, according to

Mrs Harris, who has spent a lot of time talking to them on the beach, they are the sweetest people.

'Hi guys,' Kevin says when he lopes up to the table. 'How you doing?'

'*Well*,' Mrs Harris says, thrumming her fingers on the edge of her glass, 'I don't know about you two, but we've had quite the dramatic evening.'

Mrs Harris proceeds to give her account of the abortive dog-rescue. Cheyenne watches Kevin and Laura nod and frown. She knows for a fact – because she heard Laura telling her mother – that the bed in Kevin and Laura's honeymoon suite is sprinkled nightly with rose petals. The image of this bed – of Kevin and Laura rolling around on it – fascinates her. She wonders how many times they've done it since they've been on honeymoon. Every night? Three times a night? Are they going to do it when they get back to their room this evening, all greasy-mouthed and smelling of baby back ribs?

'So this couple took Shy in,' Mrs Harris is saying, 'and they were obviously just the loveliest people because they tried everything, short of giving this dog the kiss of life. But he got sicker and sicker and in the end, he just keeled over and died right in front of them. Right in their house. Poor Shy saw it all …'

Cheyenne glances at her mother. It is irritating the way she has appropriated the story as her own and is now rattling on authoritatively about the English couple as if she had met them herself.

'They were obviously very worried about Shy. So, of course, they insisted on driving her back to the hotel—'

'No, they didn't,' Cheyenne objects. 'I told you, they got their maid to drive me back in a golf cart.'

Mrs Harris goes on as if she hadn't spoken. 'I can't tell you how glad I am they were such decent people. As a mother, you know, you worry so much. I was thinking, actually, that we should drop by their house tomorrow to thank them.'

Cheyenne's mouth forms an incredulous 'O'. The idea of her parents turning up at the couple's front door – her mother in one of her hideous sarongs, her father in his crab-motif vacation shorts – is too mortifying to be borne. 'No,' she blurts out, 'you can't, Mom.'

'Pardon?' Her mother looks at her archly.

'They wouldn't like it.'

'What are you talking about?'

'They just seemed like very private people.'

Her mother rolls her eyes and chuckles. '*Private* people. Oh my.'

'I will totally kill you, Mom, if you go to their house.'

Mr Harris places a hand on Cheyenne's arm. 'That's enough, young lady.' He looks at Kevin and Laura. 'It's been a pretty tough evening for Shy,' he says, 'watching the dog die and everything.'

'Oh, I bet,' Laura murmurs.

'Cheyenne's crazy about animals,' Mrs Harris adds proudly.

Later on that evening, Mrs Harris comes to Cheyenne's room to give her a goodnight kiss. Cheyenne is already in bed when she knocks, eating diabetic caramel chews and reading, with no particular relish, an article in *Cosmopolitan* magazine, entitled 'Twenty Ways to Turn Your Man On'. Most of the acts to which the article refers sound vile to her – so surreally repulsive, in fact, that she has a hard time believing anyone actually commits them.

Tip 16. Don't neglect the male mammaries! Go ahead and bite his nipples! If she could reject this part of adult life, she thinks – if she could simply dismiss it as something not for her, like tennis or chess club – she would. But no one, apart from nuns and total freaks, ever opts out of sex. And at school, she is already halfway to loserdom, for never having French-kissed. So she perseveres – storing up the article's appalling nuggets of information, like a squirrel gathering food for the coming winter.

'Are you okay, sweetie?' her mother says when she opens the door.

'Sure, I'm fine.'

Her mother gazes at her intently. 'I know you're broken up about the dog. I just want you to know that I'm really proud of what you did today. A lot of kids wouldn't even have bothered trying to save him.'

Cheyenne glances over her mother's shoulder into the hallway. She feels slightly fraudulent. There is, it seems to her, an increasing disparity these days between what her mother imagines will upset her and what really does. 'Yeah, well,' she says, turning away and climbing back into bed, 'it didn't make any difference, did it? The dog still died.'

'That doesn't matter,' her mother says, shaking her head emphatically, as she closes the door behind her. 'That's not the point. The important thing is, honey, you tried. You did your best. That's the most anyone can ask of you.' She sits down on the bed. 'Do you see what I'm saying?'

Cheyenne screws up her face, trying to look as if she is just now groping towards some new and complicated truth. 'Yeah ... I guess so.'

Her mother smiles. 'You want to snuggle?'

'Sure.'

'Scooch over, then.'

Cheyenne shifts to make room for her mother and then, when her mother has found her spot, she shifts back again, into her arms. Soon she will be too old for this, she thinks.

Perhaps, she is already too old. But her mother is stroking her hair and making shushing noises and, really, she is too tired to resist. It is wonderfully safe and warm lying here, pressed to her mother's chest. She can hear the thumping of her mother's heart and the industrial gurgles of her mother's digestive system. She can smell the light steam of rum punch rising from her pores. *Mommy*, she thinks, as her eyes flicker shut. *My mommy*.

The next morning, while her parents are sunbathing at the pool, Cheyenne goes for a walk down the beach. Since it is her intention to run into the English couple again, and since she would rather not be sweaty when she does so, she has completed the cardio portion of her morning workout on the hotel treadmill. She is dressed with some care, in a white towelling sundress, a pair of wedge espadrilles and the diamond stud earrings that her parents gave her for her last birthday. As she wobbles along the sand – the espadrilles are difficult to walk in, so she has to go slowly – she plots out how the encounter will go. Caroline will be coming down the steps to the beach, just as Cheyenne passes the house. Cheyenne will stop and say how pleased she is to run into her like this because she did so want to apologise for the trouble she caused last night. Caroline will assure her that it was no problem. They will both express sympathy for the poor dog. And then, at a certain moment, they will catch one another's eyes, and start to giggle. Soon they will be hooting madly with mirth. ('The look on Hugh's face when he puked!' Caroline will cry.) As their laughter finally dies away, Caroline will glance at Cheyenne with an expression of surprise and renewed interest, realising now that, for all their superficial cultural differences, she and this sparky young American have an awful lot in common. 'Call me Caro,' she will say, taking Cheyenne's hand and leading her up the stairs to the deck.

But when Cheyenne gets to the house, no one is there – or no one that she can see, at any rate. She sits on the sand for a bit, looking up at the deck and hoping for someone to come out. Thirty minutes pass and neither Caroline nor Hugh appears. She considers going up the stairs and knocking on the windows, but something tells her that this would not be wise. Eventually, she stands up, takes off the espadrilles, which have begun to pinch her feet, and goes back to the hotel.

For the next three days, Caroline and Hugh remain elusive. Every morning and every afternoon, Cheyenne walks down the beach and dawdles outside their house for half an hour, before returning home disappointed. One afternoon, when she and her parents go to the other side of the island

to look at the boats in the marina, she becomes briefly convinced that a woman water-skiing in the bay is Caroline. She
jumps up and down and waves like an idiot. But when the
boat comes closer, the woman turns out to be someone else
entirely – a younger, much coarser-looking person, with the
word 'JUICY' printed on the back of her bikini bottom.

'Well, if that's what your English woman was like,' Mrs
Harris remarks, 'I'm very glad I didn't meet her.'

On the final afternoon of her vacation, Cheyenne is dropped
off at the paved, open-air mall in town, with her father's
American Express card and the instruction that she may
purchase whatever she wants, within reason. The day is
hot and overcast and the mall is crowded with intimidating
young people, drinking beer from plastic cups and shrieking merry obscenities at one another. Cheyenne, who has
had to fight to be allowed to make this shopping trip alone,
finds herself rather anxious and disconsolate as she wanders
up and down the street, searching for souvenirs. After an
hour, she buys two T-shirts, one for herself, printed with the
slogan 'WILL WORK FOR SHOES' and another for her best
friend, Sasha, that says 'QUEEN BE-ATCH'.

On her way out of the mall, she passes a boutique called
Sea Biscuit. It is a much smarter, sleeker establishment than

any of the other shops she has looked at. There is a sign on its door telling customers to ring for admission and in its tasteful, sea-themed window display, pieces of jewellery have been scattered like flotsam across a bed of sand and seaweed. Lying at the outer edge of the display is a set of thin gold bangles just like the ones that Caroline wore.

When Cheyenne presses the bell, the answering buzz comes instantaneously. Pushing open the door, she enters a narrow, bright room, at the far end of which a skinny woman stands behind a counter, folding shirts. Too shy to ask about the bangles straight out, Cheyenne slopes about the shop, clutching her T-shirts and purse, pretending to browse. The clothes on the racks – austere linen tunics and pants in neutral shades – puzzle her. They are meant, she supposes, for older women, although it is impossible to imagine her mother ever wearing such things.

'Were you looking for anything in particular?' the woman asks at last.

Cheyenne blushes. 'I was wondering how much the gold bangles in the window were.'

The woman comes out from behind the counter and points at a glass-fronted cabinet. 'Sixty dollars.' She smiles a quick, unfriendly smile. 'Each.'

Cheyenne nods gravely, refusing to betray any surprise. 'May I look at them?'

'They're great, these,' the woman says, growing a little more animated as she unlocks the cabinet. 'You can wear them with anything and they really funk up an outfit ...'

Cheyenne tries on ten bangles and holds out her wrist to inspect them. They are beautiful, she thinks. Delicate. Feminine. When she shakes her wrist, they make a subtle tinkling noise just as Caroline's did.

'Cute, right?' the woman says.

Cheyenne takes them off and lays them on top of the cabinet. 'I'll take four, please.'

The woman nods and starts replacing the other bangles.

'No, sorry,' Cheyenne says quickly, 'I'll take six.'

Back at the hotel, Cheyenne wakes her parents from their nap to let them know that she is home safely. Her mother inspects her purchases. The bangles are beautiful, she says. 'Were they expensive?' she asks – whispering, so that Mr Harris will not hear.

Cheyenne nods sheepishly.

'Naughty girl!' her mother says, beaming. 'They really do set off your tan, you know. Look—' She pulls Cheyenne into the bathroom so that she can see for herself in the full-length mirror.

It takes a moment before the greenish overhead light flickers on. Cheyenne looks at herself: a hot, dirty-faced girl grinning expectantly as she holds up her chubby wrist. Her hair is greasy and a rim of belly flesh is pressing over the waistband of her shorts.

'Look how gorgeous!' her mother cries.

Cheyenne's arm drops to her side. How pathetic to have imagined that jewellery would transform her. How cruel of her mother to have encouraged the delusion!

She turns quickly and goes back into the bedroom to start gathering up her things.

'You want to have a shower before dinner?' her mother asks, following her out.

Cheyenne shakes her head. 'I'm going for a run.'

'Oh, not now, love. It's already getting dark. I told you I didn't want you out there after—'

Cheyenne leaves the room, slamming the door behind her.

The moon is already risen by the time she gets down to the beach. It is hanging, almost full, just above the horizon, shedding a silvery path of light across the water. Cheyenne is too disconsolate to jog. She settles for a speed-walk. As she approaches the English people's house, she slows down, preparing herself for the familiar thud of disappointment. But tonight, miraculously, someone is there.

It is Hugh, standing on the deck and waving at her. 'Come up!' he shouts.

Cheyenne silently curses the gods that sent her out this evening without her espadrilles.

'Okay!' she shouts back.

When she gets up to the deck, Hugh is sitting on the edge of the dining table, swinging his legs. He has a light growth of orange beard on his cheeks and chin. Otherwise, he looks just as he did the last time. 'You haven't brought me another dying animal, have you?' he asks languidly.

'No.'

'Thank God for that.'

Cheyenne glances around the deck. 'Where's Caroline?'

'Miami. She had a lunch do today with some of her mates.' He hops off the table. 'I was about to make myself a drink. Will you join me?'

'Sure.' She looks at him, curiously. Perhaps it was the dog that made him so bad-tempered before, she thinks. Or perhaps he is just lonely now, without his wife.

'What'll you have?' he asks.

'Whatever. Do you have a Diet Coke?'

He groans. 'I refuse to let you drink that filthy stuff. Have a Bloody Mary with me, instead.'

'I don't know what that is.'

'My goodness. We must enlighten you.'

'Does it have alcohol in it?'

'Just a bit. It's mostly tomato juice.'

'Okay, then.'

He beckons her to follow him into the house. 'Take a pew. I'll be back in a minute.'

She sits down on a sofa. Everything in the room is very clean and modern. All the furniture is white and there's not a ornament or a framed family photograph in sight. 'Space-age' – that is the phrase she will use when she describes it to her mother.

Hugh comes back, carrying the drinks on a tray. 'Here you go. Try this.' He hands her a tall glass with a stick of celery poking out of it.

'What do I do with the celery?' she asks.

'What would you like to do?'

'I don't know. Am I meant to eat it, or what?'

'People generally leave it.'

She pushes the celery to one side with her finger and takes a cautious sip.

'You like?' he says.

She nods. 'It's nice. Spicy.'

He sits down opposite her on a white wingback chair and stretches out his legs. His feet are very rough and ill-kempt. The toes actually look like they might have that fungal thing.

'What happened to the dog?' she asks.

He laughs. 'Is that a metaphysical question?'

'Sorry?'

'Do you want to know if he went to dog heaven?'

She frowns. It's annoying, the way he keeps making fun of her. 'I was just wondering what did you do with his body,' she says.

'Our gardener took him down to the south end of the island and buried him in the bush. Well – that's what I told him to do. He may have cooked him up for his dinner, for all I know.' He pauses and places a hand on her knee. 'A joke, my dear.'

'I know.'

He chuckles, removes the hand. 'So. Have you had a nice holiday? What have you been doing?'

'I don't know. Just, you know, normal stuff. Sunbathing and swimming.'

'Oh dear. You must have been frightfully bored.'

She looks into her drink, wondering indignantly what he does all day that is so fascinating.

'Haven't you met any nice young boys?'

'No,' she says primly.

'Awww. Poor Cheyenne.'

She sits up suddenly, filled with an obscure sense of alarm. 'I oughtn't to stay too long. I promised my mom that I'd be back in an hour.'

He smiles, seeming not to hear. 'Did you know you have a tick?'

'A what?'

'A tick.' He points at her thigh. 'You have a tick on you.'

'No! Where?' She grabs her leg and peers at it. Sure enough, there is a fat, black dot implanted in the flesh just above her knee. 'Oh my God,' she says, 'that's gross. I didn't know you could get ticks on this island.'

He gazes at her, amused by her consternation. 'Would you like me to get it out for you?'

'Yes! Please.'

He goes into another room and returns, holding tweezers. 'Trust me,' he says, drolly, sitting down on a low ottoman and snapping the tweezers, 'I'm a doctor.'

He begins by probing at the bulge with his finger. Cheyenne can feel his hot breath on her thigh. She lets her head fall back against the sofa and scrunches her eyes shut in an agony of embarrassment. 'Aren't you meant to put Vaseline on it first?' she asks after a moment.

'No, no – that's a myth. One of the worst things you can do. It just makes it slippery ...'

There is a sharp pinch and, a moment later, he holds up something trapped between the blades of his tweezers. 'Look at that little monster.' He drops it into his Bloody Mary glass, which, she notices now, is almost empty. 'Only thing you can do with these things – drown 'em.'

Cheyenne stares at the bloated, shining bug as it sinks slowly into the tomato juice. 'Oh, that is disgusting …'

'Perhaps,' Hugh says, 'we ought to give you a thorough checking.' He is standing now, looking down at her with a strange half smile on his face.

Cheyenne titters uneasily. She starts to tell him that she doesn't need to be checked, that she will get her mother to do it when she goes back to the hotel. Before she can finish, he leans over and thrusts his hand down the front of her shorts.

She gasps, like someone being splashed with cold water. 'What are you doing?'

He does not reply. His hand is foraging around, plucking at the tops of her underpants.

She stares down at herself, momentarily transfixed by the sight of his thick red arm plunged into her shorts. So *this* is what it is like. 'What are you doing?' she asks again.

'Oh, I think you have a rough idea,' he mutters. His face has grown very red. As he clambers on top of her, she glimpses the shiny violet insides of his ears.

'Stop it!' she cries. 'I don't want to.' She writhes about

beneath him, trying to throw him off. When his arm presses momentarily against her face, she bites down hard, feeling tendons squeak beneath her teeth.

'Fuck!' he bellows.

Just as abruptly as it started, it is over. He climbs off her now, and walks to the other side of the room, holding his injured arm tenderly in his hand. 'What extraordinary fucking behaviour,' he says. 'Why on earth did you come up here, you silly little girl?'

Cheyenne pulls herself up on the sofa, panting, clutching her groin. 'I thought …' She cannot remember now what she thought. 'You waved at me,' she says weakly. 'I wanted to find out about the dog '

'Oh, do stop that Doctor Dolittle act,' he hisses. 'You think it makes you interesting, but it doesn't, you know. It's very dull and childish.'

In an instant she is up and bolting for the door. As she leaves the house, he shouts something after her. She does not stop to find out what. She runs across the deck and all the way down the stairs, and when she reaches the beach she keeps on running.

Her face is streaming with snot and tears. She rubs at her legs and arms, trying to slough off the touch of him. She has no doubt that she is culpable for what has taken place. It is just as he said, she is a silly little girl.

She follows a line of seaweed that has been left by the outgoing tide – a long lazy cursive of bramble dotted with bottle tops and shards of coloured plastic and the odd bashed-in buoy. A brisk breeze has come up since she has been inside and lacy clouds are scudding across the evening sky. Slowly, as the distance grows between her and the house, her fear dissipates. In its place, there comes a queer sort of exhilaration. Something has happened at last. The something is ugly and shameful, but it doesn't matter. Already, she feels, the terrible burden of her innocence is a little lighter. Glancing upwards now, she has the momentary impression that it is not the clouds, but the moon, that is moving so swiftly. She pauses for a moment, admiring this trompe l'oeil – the silver orb falling dreamily through the heavens like an errant Christmas tree bauble. She wonders if her parents will notice the change in her. She pictures her mother probing and cajoling over dinner in the Pink Bar. *Everything okay, Shy? How was your run?* And then she imagines herself, smiling a gracious, shut-eyed Caro-smile, hugging her new, secret self close. She will wear her bangles, she thinks. And some mint lip gloss. And when her poached chicken comes, she will be super-good and eat only the garnish.

Bethany-next-
the-Sea

JUST BECAUSE SHE HAS a small part in a low-budget, independent film – a very small part, slightly better than an extra – Bethany Mellmoth has been strictly telling herself not to get any grand ideas and to stop fantasising, in her many moments alone, of this project as a film 'starring Bethany Mellmoth'. Only bitter disappointment lies that way, Bethany repeats to herself, wondering what the poster will look like. One of the reasons she finds herself thinking about the poster is that the title of the film keeps changing. When she was first sent the script in London it was called 'Paradise (Lost)'. When she was met by the unit runner at Norwich station and handed the new, much thinner draft it was entitled 'God v. Satan', as if it were a horror/action movie. Now she sees from her call-sheet for tomorrow that it is known as 'JM@PL.com' – most off-putting. When she first read the script it was the story about a young schizophrenic called John Milton, living in contemporary London, who believes he is possessed by the spirit of the 17th century poet and that answers to all his mental problems are to be found in the text of *Paradise Lost*. Now all the contemporary scenes have been withdrawn while they are rewritten and they are only shooting the period flashback sections. Bethany supposes that Gareth Gonzalez Wintle, as he's both the director and the writer, knows what he is doing. She looks at her watch – only 2.45 – a long time to go before she can cook her frugal supper and even longer before she can decently go to the pub. There is only one thing for it – another walk on the beach. She takes three paces to the end of the caravan and feels it tip slightly under her weight, like a boat, and rummages in her suitcase (never fully unpacked) for her book, *Paradise Lost* by John Milton. There's no point in taking her script because her character has no lines – even though she was promised lines – just stage directions that bear no relation to the set or location or what she is ever asked to do by Gareth Gonzalez Wintle. She checks her bag – phone, purse, cigarettes, lighter, lipsalve, notebook, camera, peppermints, Buddha mascot. She pulls on her red Wellington boots, coat, scarf and beanie-cap, finds the keys to the caravan and steps out the door, locking it behind her – a merely symbolic gesture, she thinks, as the door seems so flimsy and thin, even she would be able to punch or kick a hole in it if she had burglary on her mind. She pauses and lights a cigarette, noting simultaneously that she only has three left – she'll have to buy some more – and that she's smoking too much on this film. Her mother has promised to give her £1000 if she stops smoking before her twenty-fourth birthday but the sum seems unreal, a chimera, unobtainable. She exhales, audibly, feeling her mood darken, angry at her weak will, frustrated at how everything seems to be going wrong in minor, aggravating, inconsequential ways – such as the caravan and its disadvantages – not significant or provocative enough to generate the key decision to leave and start again, she considers. She has small, nagging grumbles, not real complaints or problems, and she would feel ashamed turning up at home having left the film for such footling, silly reasons – squandering this amazing opportunity, this once-in-a-lifetime chance to really make it as a film actress. Or at least start to make it.

The caravan park at Faith-next-the-Sea in Norfolk sits midway between the town with its small inland harbour and the sea itself, almost a mile distant. Faith-quite-far-from-Sea should be its name, Bethany thinks, as she plods along the road to the beach beside the narrow-gauge railway towards the shuttered, brightly coloured beach cabins and the vast, endless stretch of sand that low tide has revealed. She already feels her spirits lifting as she approaches the beach and the distant sound of surf begins to whisper in her ears. It's a grey blustery day for September, more like February or March, she thinks, glad of her coat and scarf. One hour up the beach, she says to herself, one hour back, telly, beans on toast, drink in the pub, early to bed ready for the six o'clock call for hair and make-up. An actor's life has its compensations, she decides – and she's getting paid, she must remember, £50 a day plus free accommodation.

Bethany stands in the middle of the enormous, apparently endless beach surrounded by square miles of damp sand, the surf still some hundred yards off, the light pearly and uniform, the horizon a blurry, darker grey line shading into the clouds. Turning, she sees the black-green jagged stripe of the pines behind the dunes and, beyond that, more unchanging grey sky. A kind of dizziness afflicts her – she senses her insignificance, a small two-legged homunculus in the midst of all this space, a mere speck, a tiny crawling gnat in this elemental simplicity of sand, water and sky. She squats on her haunches, worried she might fall over, and to distract herself takes out her camera and frames a shot of the beach, the sea and the packed clouds – it looks like an abstract painting. Click. It looks like an abstract painting by – what was his name? Colour-field paintings, they are called, the three layers of colour-fields in this case being broad, horizontal bands of dark taupe, slate grey, nebulous tarnished silver. It is rather beautiful. She stands up, feeling equilibrium return – maybe she was hungry and felt faint for a second or two, or maybe, she wonders, maybe she has experienced an actual existential moment – an epiphany – and has seen clearly the reality of her place in the world and has felt the nothingness, the vast indifference of the universe …

Gareth Gonzalez Wintle rehearses the scene in front of camera. Howard Duke is playing John Milton with primitive small dark sunglasses, like black pennies mounted on a simple wire frame. These glasses are Duke's idea, Bethany knows, as she overheard the argument Gareth had with him, trying vainly to persuade him that they were anachronistic. Duke is also playing Milton with a thick Cockney accent – his idea, as well. 'He was born in Cheapside, for fuck's sake, Gareth,' Duke said. 'He's a Lahndaner, mate.' Gareth had conceded the point. If she is honest, Bethany is a little frightened of Howard Duke. Out of character, he has a deep, plummy voice and an impassive, immobile face, hardly moving his lips when he speaks. He refers to Bethany, whenever he rarely has to, as 'Sweets'. Bethany affects a feigned cool around him – as if unimpressed by his reputation, indifferent to his fame – that possibly explains why she is smoking so much.

Bethany is baffled by this scene. She is playing a maid in the Milton household called 'Amy Coster' and she interrupts the great poet as he is dictating the opening lines of *Paradise Lost* to Andrew Marvell (the singer-songwriter Wayne Hutton, no less). Milton suppresses his huge irritation, looks up and says, 'Is that you, Amy?' At which point Bethany simply nods and, in response to Milton's next question – 'How is the day, my child?' – still says nothing. The problem Bethany has is that Milton then responds, 'Aye, you're right, methought there was rain coming. It'll be here by noontide.' Then Bethany/Amy leaves and Milton carries on with his epic poem.

At lunch – curried eggs and chips – Bethany wonders whether she should bring this matter up with Gareth. She sees him scraping his uneaten eggs into the bin-liner hanging on the rear of the catering van and seizes the moment.

'Gareth? Got a sec?'

'Yeah, hi, Melanie, cool, how are you?'

'Bethany.'

'Sorry. Sorry – fuckwit. Nightmare day. Bethany, Bethany, Bethany.' He repeats her name a few more times like a mantra. He does look tired, Bethany thinks, his eyes red and sore, his face unshaven. He would be quite a good-looking guy if his chin wasn't slightly weak. Bethany explains her dilemma. If Milton is blind, how can he see her nod when he asks if it is Amy? Furthermore, shouldn't she say something when he wonders what the weather is like? His answer seems to imply that she's said something so shouldn't—

'Don't worry, Bethany. We'll sort it out in post.'

'I could just say, "It looks like rain, sire," or something.'

'We've finished that scene. It's in the can.'

'But it seems stupid—'

'Stupid?'

'Well, illogical.'

'Details, Bethany. Don't bother me with fucking details! I've got a fucking movie to make here!'

To her annoyance, Bethany then has a brief cry in the Portaloo. Gareth had thrown his plate and cutlery into the bin-liner and strode off muttering to himself. She could see how angry he was and she knows that he is under pressure – this is his first feature film. It doesn't matter how many commercials or rock videos you've made, a full-length period feature film is a different animal – a snarling, hairy, unruly beast longing to create mayhem. There's a knock on the door and she hears Howard Duke's drawling voice.

'Is there a cholera epidemic going on in there?'

She steps out, trying to manufacture an ironic smile.

'Sorry.'

'You all right, Sweets?'

'Yeah. Absolutely fine. How're you?'

It's at moments like these, at the end of the filming day, that Bethany misses Layla, her erstwhile caravan co-dweller. Layla Gravell played Milton's wife 'Mary', a role with a few lines. She and Bethany shared the caravan at Faith-next-the-Sea for four days before Layla walked off the set, packed and went back to Swansea, where she lived. Before she left, she advised Bethany to quit also. 'Of all the half-arsed, sad-sack, loser films I've worked on, this one takes the biscuit,' she said in her husky sing-song accent. So she went away and Bethany moved into her slightly more comfortable divan-bed. Milton's wife Mary is written out of the film.

Bethany comes back from the pub a bit drunk. She played pool with two Faith lads and beat them, to their incredulous chagrin. They bought her two double vodkas and cranberry juice – the bet – and she feels their effect now as she bangs around the galley kitchen trying to fill the kettle, light a ciga-rette and plug in the toaster. There's a knock on the door. It's

Gareth. He has a bottle of red wine in his hand and Bethany lets him in. He's here to apologise, he says, for losing his temper at lunch. He's really sorry – it was unprofessional and, worse, uncool.

'No worries, Gareth, I know you're under a lot of pressure.'

'You wouldn't believe it, mate,' Gareth says, pouring out a glass of wine and beginning to list the astonishing pressures he faces, 24/7. The more wine Gareth drinks, the angrier he becomes and the more candid. Bethany learns that the film is being financed largely by Howard Duke and a few of his wealthy friends. Gareth wrote the script, but now Duke is having it rewritten by a writer he knows called Chaz Charles.

'I don't mind being rewritten,' Gareth says, lighting one of Bethany's cigarettes. 'Don't get me wrong, Bethany – that's the movie biz, the nature of the beast. But I do mind my film about John Milton being torn apart by a pillock who writes sketches for washed-up comics and talk-show hosts.'

'Hence the title changes.'

'Exactamundo.'

'Why does Howard Duke want to play John Milton?' Bethany asks.

'Because he's sick of playing cops. He's sick of being Chief Superintendent Daniel Speed. He wants to prove he's a genuine thesp. So we meet and I pitch him my John Milton 'Paradise Lost' idea. He loves it, I write the script and then it all goes down the toilet.'

Gareth starts to rant again, standing up and pacing up and down the short length of the caravan. Gareth being heavier than Bethany, the tilt and drop as he reaches the unsteady end is more marked. Bethany instinctively realises that this is a monologue not to be interrupted, so to pass the time she writes down – on the notepad she uses for her shopping lists – all the words Gareth uses to illustrate his troubles. Howard Duke and Chaz Charles are the targets for most of his bile and also a man called Terry Arbuthnot whom Duke has brought in as a producer. Amongst the many adjectives Bethany writes down, she sees that 'dull' is a particular favourite – also 'banal', 'mulish', 'vapid', 'nauseating', 'suburban', 'drab', 'gutless', 'mediocre', 'ugly', 'trivial', 'futile', 'odious', 'provincial', 'petty', 'constipated', 'lazy', 'infuriating', 'stale' and 'stupid' – as well as many assorted swear words. Gareth empties the bottle of wine.

'I sit there listening to these ghastly, trivial nonentities, trying to conceal the wracking spasms of contempt I feel for their drab little turnip brains as they mumble on about John Milton and *Paradise Lost*. It's Kafkaesque. I mean, I went to Cambridge University and got a perfectly acceptable degree in English Literature, and I have to kowtow to Terry Arbuthnot, a property developer who made his money from, from, from, I don't know ... shopping centres and multi-storey car parks, suggesting that it would be "sexier" if Andrew Marvell was a woman.'

Bethany feels a form of supernatural exhaustion creep over her as he talks on, grateful that she has a day off tomorrow. Gareth eventually asks if she has any more drink and, when she says no, he decides he'd better be on his way. He kisses her on both cheeks and gives her a hug as he leaves. He steps out into the caravan park and looks around him in astonishment, as if he's noticing the caravans for the first time.

'Why the hell are you living here, anyway?' he says.

'This is where they put me.'

'No, no, no, we've got to get you into the hotel with the rest of the cast and crew. Leave it to me.' He wanders off into the night.

The next day, keen for it to pass as quickly as possible, Bethany takes a bus from Faith-next-the-Sea along the coast to Hunstanton. 'Hunston,' the bus driver corrects her pronunciation when she pays for her ticket, 'Sunny Hunny'. She wanders around the town and buys herself a sandwich and can of Coke. She takes a photograph of the curious striped cliffs with their horizontal bands of white and red chalk making them look like some kind of giant cake. It is a cool hazy day and she peers vainly across the Wash, failing to make out the Lincolnshire shore. Given the weather conditions she decides against a boat trip to Seal Island to seal-watch and finds herself a sheltered corner, where she sends texts to various people. To her mother; to her father and stepmother, Chen-Chi, in Los Angeles ('Movie going great!'); to her girl friends – Moxy, Jez and Arabella. She also sends a blunt text to her so-called boyfriend, Kasimierz, who has promised to come and visit her on set but seems to be the busiest man in London. She has been looking forward to them playing house (and making love) in the tilting Faith-next-the-Sea caravan but he seems determined to disappoint her. 'Two days left. The clock is ticking. B.' is all she sends him. Everyone else replies over the course of the afternoon except Kasimierz – which casts her down somewhat. It's drizzling when she reaches the bus stop and she smokes two cigarettes as she waits with four old ladies for the bus back along the coast. They stare at her as if she's some kind of alien.

It's dusk when she reaches the caravan park, and as she's walking towards her caravan she meets Gareth Gonzalez Wintle coming the other way.

'Hey, Bethany,' he says. 'I've been knocking on your door for five minutes, I was convinced you were inside. All the lights were on.'

They decide to go to the pub for a quick drink. Two hours later Bethany is still listening to Gareth's complaints – 'horror', 'arid', 'maggoty', 'cock-crowing egomaniacs', 'repulsive', 'mental dwarves', 'jaded sense of futility' are some of the words and phrases she logs away.

Eventually she asks him, 'Gareth, was there something you wanted to tell me?'

'Ah ... yeah. You are a fantastically beautiful young woman.'

'Not that.'

'I love your long hair, your lips, your green eyes. Blueish-grey eyes.' Gareth has had four gin and tonics by now.

'Not that. Why did you come to my caravan?'

'We wrapped early. Felt like a chat. You're a very easy person to talk to, Bethany. No, I was just feeling kinda ... down, low. Yeah? I'm thinking of chucking it all in after this piece-of-shit film. Clearing out.'

'To Spain?'

He looks at her, baffled.

'Why would I go to Spain?'

'I don't know. Your name, I suppose. I assumed you were half-Spanish – Gonzalez.'

'Oh. No, I'm English. I'm from Surrey. I just stuck Gonzalez in to make me sound more interesting. "A Gareth Wintle film", "A film by Gareth Wintle" – doesn't work. No way.'

'What's wrong with being called Gareth Wintle?'

'Because I sound like ... like a weather-forecaster. Like a children's TV host. An ink-stained clerk in a Dickens novel. Gareth Gonzalez Wintle – whole different ball game.'

Bethany says she has to get back. Gareth suggests buying a bottle of wine and having a night-cap. Bethany is firm.

'No thanks, Gareth. My big day tomorrow.'

'What? ... Oh, yeah ...'

Bethany sits in her costume on the lower floor of the double-decker cafeteria bus where they eat their meals waiting for the second assistant director (a harassed girl called Frankie) to come and fetch her on set. Bethany is wearing a shapeless grey coarse-wool dress with an apron, wooden clogs, and her hair is coiled and pinned up under a cloth bonnet, her face plain and scrubbed. She is remarkably calm, she thinks, given that she is about to play her one big scene in this film. In it she enters John Milton's study with a basket of logs for the fire. Milton is asleep in his armchair. The complete manuscript of *Paradise Lost* is placed on a stool by his side.

A small coal from the fire spits out and lands on the manuscript, where it smoulders, smoke rising. Amy Coster steps forward and plucks it off, burning her fingers in the process. She stifles her cry of pain and tiptoes out of the parlour, so quietly that Milton snoozes on, unaware. Amy knows she's saved her master's work from burning – we, the audience, realise how close posterity came to losing the greatest epic poem in English literature, but for the quick thinking of an illiterate chambermaid, or so it says in the script. Bethany wonders how Gareth will film it – something tricksy, no doubt, she supposes: the coal spitting from the fire in slow motion, a whip-pan round to see Amy enter, the sizzle of burning flesh as she picks up the ember ...

She stops herself, Gareth has come in. He puts on what she can only describe as a sickly smile.

'Hey, Bethany. Bit of a slight change of plan ...'

Bethany would have liked to leave at once, but by the time she has changed out of her costume, been to the accountant to be paid and is ready to be driven back to the caravan, she is told by Frankie that the unit car will pick her up at nine the next morning to take her to Norwich station. She packs her things away in her suitcase and goes to the pub, where she drinks two double vodkas and cranberry juice and eats a steak and kidney pie with chips followed by apple crumble. She's pleased that not once has she felt like crying, even at the moment when Gareth told her that her scene was cancelled. The whole film is changing, he said – bullishly, unapologetically – yeah, Howard isn't happy, isn't a happy camper. Chaz Charles has come up with a significant re-write. The young schizophrenic John Milton is changing to Detective Inspector John Milton, a charismatic cop following up a serial killer who leaves clues taken from *Paradise Lost* on the bodies of his victims – the whole flashback period part of the film is being majorly reduced. The title is now 'Lost Exit to Paradise'.

Bethany, feeling very full, walks back to the caravan park from the pub analysing her mood – cold anger, she would say. Mature resignation. A certain cynicism. A worldly acknowledgement about how easy it is to be let down in this life.

Her cold anger intensifies when she sees Gareth 'Gonzalez' Wintle waiting outside her caravan.

'I don't have anything to say to you, Gareth.'

'I want to apologise, Bethany. Just five minutes.'

She lets him in and they sit facing each other across the scratched Formica of the fold-down snack table.

'It stinks, this business,' he says, with what seems like real bitterness. 'That's why I'm getting out. I'm taking your advice.'

'What advice?'

'I'm going to Spain.'

'Great. Anyway, no hard feelings, Gareth. I just wish you'd told me last night instead of letting me come in, go to wardrobe and make up, then sit around like a complete prat preparing myself, when everybody knew – except me. This is my first film.'

'I know, I know, I'm weak, Bethany. Weak. Craven. And I was distracted. By you. I was enjoying being with you.'

'Yeah, well, I've got to pack,' Bethany lies.

'Listen. You'll be in the film. I'll make sure of that. I'll make sure you get a credit, as well.' He gestures out the names, horizontally, with thumb and forefinger. 'Amy Coster – Bethany Mellmoth. You'll get your Equity card. It'll look good in Spotlight, put it on your CV.'

That would be something, at least, Bethany thinks, reaching for her cigarettes – but Gareth intercepts her outstretched hand, taking it in both his.

'You won't have wasted your time, Bethany,' he says. He brings her hand to his lips, smiles at her, kisses her knuckles. 'Can I stay the night?'

Bethany can't sleep. Her crowding thoughts won't let her. So as soon as she sees it growing light outside, she dresses,

pulls on her Wellingtons and coat and scarf and goes for a
final walk on the beach.

The tide is out and she walks hundreds of yards down
the wet sand to the surf's edge. The light is ghostly, mono-
chrome, almost as if she's in a black-and-white photograph
– the black sea, the silvery grey clouds, the beach shining,
nacreous, softly gilded by the shrouded, rising sun. When
she told Gareth to get out and told him how pathetic, suburban and nauseating she thought he was, how gutless,
vapid and maggoty, he had sneered at her at first, laughed,
and then, to her alarm, had teared-up and turned away,
then sniffed and tossed his head and said in a small, suddenly hoarse voice that he just wanted to be with someone
he liked, how he hated everyone on the film except Bethany,
no big deal, no sex required, just company. She held the
door open for him and he asked if he could kiss her goodbye. So she let him kiss her cheek, shook his hand, said she
would see him in London once the film was over, and he
walked away.

Bethany sets off, heading north up the beach, allowing
the foamy wavelets to wet her boots. My god, she thinks –
get real, girl. 'Paradise Lost starring Bethany Mellmoth'. She
pauses, turns to face the black, restless sea and spreads her
arms, shouting at the top of her voice:

'Of man's first disobedience and the fruit

Of that forbidden tree, whose mortal truth
Brought death into the world, and all our woe ...'

Her voice sounds small and lonely, she thinks, so she
stops, hearing only the wave-crash and the distant cry of
gulls, and she has another of those being-and-nothingness
moments that makes her shiver. Time to go home, to the
caravan to have a cup of coffee and some toast and marma-
lade. She turns and strides back towards Faith-next-the-Sea
but she's only gone a few paces when she sees something
that makes her change direction. It's a dead seagull, left by
the retreating tide, she supposes, white, grey and seemingly
untouched, lying on its back, one wing out, one wing folded,
its head tipped to one side as if it was sleeping. It looks
very pure and beautiful, she thinks, and reaches into her
bag for her camera, very calm and composed. She takes a
photograph, inspired by the seagull's transcendent stillness,
the unblemished smooth whiteness of its breast feath-
ers. There's a play called *The Seagull* she remembers. Who
wrote it? She wanders homeward, up the beach towards
her caravan, urging her brain to come up with the author.
That's right, Chekhov, Anton Chekhov. Perhaps it's a sign,
she thinks, a symbol that she shouldn't give up her acting
career. Just because her first film has been such a disaster
doesn't mean she should pack it all in. No, she is destined
to be an actress, she's sure – but if the cinema won't have

her there is always the theatre. The theatre, she thinks, the West End, Shaftesbury Avenue ... *The Seagull* by Anton Chekhov, starring Bethany Mellmoth ... She walks up the beach towards Faith-next-the-Sea, pondering this exciting alternative future for herself, her stride lengthening with new enthusiasm, then she finds herself skipping – actually skipping along the sand – something she hasn't done since she was a child.

Walking After Midnight

This is an excerpt from a novel in progress,
The Book of Strange New Things,
set in a very, very foreign place.
The hero is a Christian missionary.

MICHEL FABER (born Den Haag, Netherlands, 1960) grew up in
Australia, where, after university, he worked as a nurse. He has lived
in Scotland since 1993. He has produced seven books, all published in
the UK by Canongate, including *Under the Skin*, *The Crimson Petal and the
White* and *The Fire Gospel*. 'Walking After Midnight' is a specially adapted
excerpt from a novel in progress. The finished book will be even more
relevant to Oxfam's concerns than this excerpt suggests.

PETER SLEPT, AND AWOKE to the sound of rain.

For a long time he lay in the dark, too tired to stir, listening. The rain sounded different from rain back home. Its intensity waxed and waned in a rapid cyclical rhythm, three seconds at most between surges. He synchronised the fluctuations with his own breathing, inhaling when the rain fell softer, exhaling when it fell hard. What made the rain do that? Was it natural, or was it caused by the design of the building: a wind-trap, an exhaust fan, a faulty portal opening and closing? Could it be something as mundane as his own window flapping in the breeze? He could see no further than the slats of the Venetian blind.

Eventually his curiosity got the better of his fatigue. He staggered out of bed, fumbled for the bathroom light, was momentarily blinded by halogen overkill. He squinted at his watch, the only item of apparel he'd kept on when he'd gone to bed. Damn: he'd slept only seven hours ... unless he'd slept thirty-one. He checked the date. No, only seven. What had woken him? His erection, perhaps.

The bathroom was in all respects identical to a bathroom one might expect to find in a corporate hotel, except that the toilet, instead of employing a simple flush mechanism, was the kind that sucked out its contents in a whoosh of compressed air. Peter pissed slowly and with some discomfort, waiting for his penis to unstiffen. His urine was dark orange. Alarmed, he filled a glass with water from the faucet. The liquid was pale green. Clean and transparent, but pale green. Stuck to the wall above the sink was a printed notice: 'COLOR OF WATER IS GREEN. THIS IS NORMAL AND CERTIFIED SAFE. IF IN DOUBT, BOTTLED WATER & SOFT DRINKS ARE AVAILABLE, SUBJECT TO AVAILABILITY, FROM USIC STORE, $50 PER 300ml'.

Peter drank a glass of green water, having briefly considered how God might wish him to proceed. The only two scripture quotations which came to his mind, 'Take no thought for what ye shall drink' from *Matthew 6:25* and 'To the pure, all things are pure' from *Titus 1:15*, were clearly meant for other contexts. In any case, he had no choice. Not being a USIC employee, he couldn't elect to have the cost of bottled water deducted from his wages.

The water tasted good. Divine, in fact. Was that a blasphemous thought? 'Oh, give it a rest,' his wife would no doubt advise him. 'There are more important things in the world to fret about.' What things might there be to fret about in this world? He would find out soon enough. He stood up, flushed the toilet, drank more of the green water. It tasted faintly of honeydew melon, or maybe he was only imagining that.

Still naked, he walked to the bedroom window. There must be a way of raising the blind, even though there were no switches or buttons in sight. He felt around the edges of the slats, and his fingers snagged in a cord. He tugged on it and the blind lifted. It occurred to him as he continued pulling on the cord that he might be exposing his nakedness to anyone who happened to be passing by, but it was too late to worry about that now. The window – one large pane of Plexiglas – was wholly revealed.

Outside, darkness still ruled. The area surrounding the USIC airport complex was a wasteland (the word 'god-forsaken' came to mind), a dead zone of featureless tarmac, dismal shed-like buildings, and spindly steel lamps. It was like a supermarket car park that went on forever. And yet Peter's heart pumped hard, and he breathed shallowly in his excitement. The rain! The rain wasn't falling in straight lines; it was ... dancing! Could one say that about rainfall? Water had no intelligence. And yet, this rainfall swept from side to side, hundreds of thousands of silvery lines all describing the same elegant arcs. It was nothing like when rain back home was flung around erratically by gusts of wind. No, the air here seemed calm, and the rain's motion was graceful, a leisurely sweeping from one side of the sky to the other – hence the rhythmic spattering against his window.

He pressed his forehead to the glass. It was blessedly cool. He realised he was running a slight fever, wondered if he was hallucinating the curvature of the rainfall. Peering out into the dark, he made an effort to focus on the hazes of light around the lampposts. Inside these halo-like spheres of illumination, the raindrops were picked out bright as tinfoil confetti. Their sensuous, undulating pattern could not be clearer.

Peter stepped back from the window. His reflection was ghostly, criss-crossed by the unearthly rain. His normally rosy-cheeked, cheerful face had a haunted look, and the tungsten glow of a distant lamppost blazed inside his abdomen. His genitals had the sculptured, alabaster appearance of Greek statuary. He raised his hand, to break the spell, to reorient himself to his own familiar humanity. But it might as well have been a stranger waving back.

Peter loitered around his quarters for a while, at a loss for what to do next. The USIC representative who'd escorted him off the ship had made all the correct noises about being available for him should he need anything. But she hadn't specified how this availability would work. Had she even

divulged her name? Peter couldn't recall. There certain,
wasn't any note left lying on the table, to welcome him, giv
him a few pointers and tell him how to get in touch.

He opened the fridge, verified that the empty ice cube
tray was the only thing in it. An apple wouldn't have been
too much to expect, would it? Or perhaps it would. He kept
forgetting how far from home he was.

It was time to go out and face that.

He got dressed in the clothes he'd worn yesterday – underpants, jeans, flannel shirt, denim jacket, socks, lace-up
shoes. He combed his hair, had another drink of greenish
water. His empty stomach gurgled and grunted, having pro-
cessed and eliminated the noodle meal he'd eaten millions
of miles before. He strode to the door; hesitated, sank to his
knees, bowed his head in prayer. He had not yet thanked
God for delivering him safe to his destination; he thanked
Him now. He thanked Him for some other things, too, but
then got the distinct feeling that Jesus was standing at his
back, prodding him, good-humouredly accusing him of stall-
ing. So he sprang to his feet and left at once.

The USIC airport mess hall was humming, not with human activity, but with recorded music. It was a large room,
one wall of which consisted almost wholly of glass, and the

music hung around it like a fog, piped from vents in the ceiling. Apart from a vague impression of watery glitter on the window, the rain outside was felt rather than seen; it added a sense of cosy, muffled enclosure to the hall.

'I stopped to see a weeping willow
Crying on his pillow
Maybe he's crying for me ...'

sang a ghostly female voice, seemingly channelled through miles of subterranean tunnels to emerge at last from an accidental aperture.

'And as the skies turn gloomy,
Night blooms whisper to me,
I'm lonesome as I can be ...'

There were four USIC employees in the mess hall, all of them young men unknown to Peter. One, an overweight, crew-cut oriental, dozed in an armchair next to a well-stocked magazine rack, his face slumped over a fist. One was working at the coffee bar, his tall spindly body draped with an oversize T-shirt emblazoned 'USIC: BRINGING IT ALL BACK HOME'. He was intently fiddling with a touch-sensitive screen balanced on the counter, poking at it with a metal pencil. He chewed at his swollen lips with large white teeth. His hair was heavy with some sort of gelatinous hair-care product. He looked Slavic. The other two men were black. They were seated at one of the tables, studying a book together. It was too large and slim to be a Bible; more likely a technical manual. At their elbows were large transparent mugs of coffee and a couple of small dessert plates, bare apart from some crumbs. Peter could smell no food in the room.

'I go out walking after midnight,
Out in the moonlight.
Just hoping you may be ...'

The three awake men noted his arrival with a nod of low-key welcome but did not otherwise interrupt what they were doing. The snoozing Asian and the two men with the book were all dressed the same: loose Middle Eastern-style shirt, loose cotton trousers, no socks, and chunky sports shoes. Islamic basketball players.

'Hi, I'm Peter,' said Peter, fronting up to the counter. 'I'm new here. I'd love something to eat, if you've got it.'

The Slavic-looking young man shook his prognathous face slowly to and fro.

'Too late, bro.'

'Too late?'

'24-hourly stock appraisal, bro. Began an hour ago.'

'I was told by the USIC people that food is provided whenever we need it.'

'Correct, bro. You just gotta make sure you don't need it at the wrong time.'

Peter digested this for a moment. The female voice on

the PA system had come to the end of her song. A male announcement followed, sonorous and insincerely intimate.

'You're listening to *Night Blooms*, a documentary chronicle of Patsy Cline's performances of 'Walkin' After Midnight' from 1957 right through to the posthumous duets in 1999. Well, listeners, did you do what I asked? Did you hold in your memory the girlish shyness, the slightly overwhelmed sense of being unworthy, that radiated from Patsy's voice in the version she performed for her debut on Arthur Godfrey's *Talent Scouts*? What a difference eleven months makes! The second version you've just heard was recorded on December 14, 1957, for the Grand Ol' Opry. By then, she clearly had more of an inkling of the song's uncanny power. But the aura of wisdom and unbearable sadness that you'll hear in the next version owes something to personal tragedy, too. On June 14, 1961, Patsy was almost killed in a head-on car collision. Incredibly, only a few days after she left hospital, we find her performing 'After Midnight' at the Cimarron Ballroom in Tulsa, Oklahoma. Listen, people, listen closely, and you will hear the pain of that terrible auto accident, the grief she must have felt at the deep scars on her forehead, which never healed ...'

The ghostly female voice wafted across the ceiling once more.

'I go out walking after midnight,
Out in the moonlight just like we used to do.

130

I'm always walking after midnight,
Searching for you ...'

'When is the next food delivery?' asked Peter.

'Food's already here, bro,' said the Slavic man, patting the counter. 'Released for consumption in ...' (he consulted the computer screen) '... six hours and twenty-seven minutes.'

'I'm sorry, I'm new here; I didn't know about this system. And I really am very hungry. Couldn't you ... uh ... release something early, and just mark it as having been served in six hours from now?'

The Slav narrowed his eyes.

'That would be ... committing an untruth, bro.'

Peter smiled and hung his head in defeat. Patsy Cline sang, *Well, that's just my way of saying I love you ...* as he walked away from the counter and sat down in one of the armchairs near the magazine rack, directly behind the sleeping man.

As soon as his back sank into the upholstery he felt exhausted and he knew that if he didn't get up again quite soon he would fall asleep. He leaned towards the magazines, taking a quick mental inventory of the selection. *Cosmopolitan, Freshwater Angler, Men's Health, Your Dog, Vogue, Dirty Sperm Whores, House & Garden, Autosport, Science Digest, Super Food Ideas* ... Pretty much the full range, it seemed. Well-thumbed and only slightly out of date.

'Hey, preacher!'

He turned in his chair. The two black men sharing the table had shut their book, finished with it for the night. One of them was holding aloft a foil-wrapped object the size of a tennis ball, wiggling it demonstratively. As soon as he had Peter's attention, he tossed the object across the room. Peter caught it easily, without even a hint of a fumble. He had always been an excellent catcher. The two black men raised a friendly fist each, congratulating him. He unwrapped the foil, found a hunk of blueberry muffin.

'Thank you!' His voice sounded strange in the acoustics of the mess hall, competing with the DJ who had resumed his exegesis of Patsy Cline, who by this stage of the narrative had perished in a plane crash.

'... personal belongings left behind after the sale of her home. The tape passed from hand to hand, unrecognised for the treasure it was, before finally ending up stored in the closet of a Florida jeweller for several years. Imagine it, friends! Those divine sounds you just heard, dormant inside an unassuming reel of magnetic tape, locked up in a dark closet, perhaps never to see the light of day. But we can be eternally grateful that the jeweller eventually woke up and negotiated a deal with MCA Records ...'

The blueberry muffin was delicious; among the best things Peter had ever tasted. And how sweet it was, too, to know that he was in not altogether hostile territory.

'Welcome to Heaven, preacher!' called one of his bene-
factors, and everyone except the sleeping Asian laughed.

Peter turned to face them, beamed them a smile. 'Well,
things are certainly looking up from what they were a few
minutes ago.'

'Onwards and upwards, preach! That's the USIC motto,
more or less.'

'So,' said Peter, 'do you guys like it here?'

The black man who'd thrown the muffin went pensive,
considering the question seriously. 'It's OK, man. As good
as anywhere.'

'Weather's cool,' his companion chipped in.

'He means the weather's warm.'

'Which is cool, man, is what I'm saying.'

'You know, I haven't even been outside yet,' said Peter.

'Oh, you should go,' said the first man, as though ac-
knowledging the possibility that Peter might prefer to spend
his entire Oasis sojourn inside his quarters. 'Check it out
before the light comes up.'

Peter stood up. 'I'd like that. Where's ... uh ... the nearest door?'

The coffee bar attendant pointed a long, bony finger past
an illuminated plastic sign that said 'ENJOY!' in large letters
and, underneath in smaller print, 'EAT AND DRINK RESPONSIBLY.
REMEMBER THAT BOTTLED WATER, CARBONATED SOFT DRINKS, CAKES,

CONFECTIONERY AND YELLOW-STICKERED ITEMS ARE NOT INCLUDED IN THE FOOD AND DRINK ALLOWANCE AND WILL BE DEDUCTED FROM YOUR EARNINGS'.

To which someone had added, in felt-tip pen:

"ENJOY' ANYWAY – SUCKERS'

'Thanks for the tip,' said Peter, as he was leaving. 'And the food!'

'Have a good one, bro.'

The last thing he heard was Patsy Cline's voice, this time in a celebrity duet recorded, through the miracle of modern technology, decades after her death.

Peter stepped through the sliding door into the air of Oasis and, contrary to an irrational apprehension, he did not instantly die, get sucked into an airless vortex, or shrivel up like a scrap of fat on a griddle. Instead, he was enveloped in a moist, warm breeze, a swirling balm that felt like steam except that it didn't make his throat catch. He strolled into the dark, his way unlit except by several distant lamps. In the dreary environs of the USIC airport, there was nothing much to see anyway, just acres of wet black tarmac, but he'd wanted to walk outside, and so here he was, walking, outside.

The sky was dark, dark aquamarine. There were only a few dozen stars visible, far fewer than he was used to, but each one shone brightly, without any flicker, and with a pale green aura. There was no moon.

The rain had stopped now, but the atmosphere still seemed substantially composed of water. If he closed his eyes, he could almost imagine he'd waded into a warm swimming pool. The air lapped against his cheeks, tickled his ears, flowed over his lips and hands. It penetrated his clothing, breathing into the collar of his shirt and down his backbone, making his shoulderblades and chest dewy, making his shirtcuffs adhere to his wrists. The warmth – it was extreme warmth rather than heat – caused his skin to prickle with sweat, making him intimately aware of his armpit hair, the clefts of his groin, the shape of his toes swaddled inside their humid footwear.

He was dressed all wrong. Those USIC guys with their loose Arabic duds had it sussed, didn't they? He would have to emulate them as soon as possible.

As he walked, he tried to sort out which unusual phenomena were occurring inside of him and which were external. His heart was beating a little faster than usual; he put that down to excitement. His gait was a little wonky, as though skewed by alcohol; he wondered if he was merely still suffering the after-effects of The Jump, jet lag and general exhaustion. His feet seemed to bounce slightly with every step, as though the tarmac was rubberised. He knelt for a moment and rapped on the ground with his knuckles. It was hard, unyielding. He stood up, and the action of standing seemed to him easier than it should be. An ever-so-slight trampoline effect. But this was counterbalanced by the watery density of the air. He lifted his hand, pushed his palm forward into space, testing for resistance. There was none, and yet the air swirled around his wrist and up his forearm, tickling him. He didn't know whether he liked it, or found it creepy. Atmosphere, in his experience, had always been an absence. The air here was a presence, a presence so palpable that he was tempted to believe he could let himself fall and the air would simply catch him like a pillow. It wouldn't, of course. But as it nuzzled against his skin, it almost seemed to promise that it would.

He took a deep breath, concentrating on the texture of it as it went in. It felt and tasted no different from normal air. He knew from the USIC brochures that the composition was much the same mix of nitrogen and oxygen he'd been breathing all his life, with a bit less carbon dioxide and a bit more ozone and a few trace elements he might not have had before. The brochures hadn't mentioned the water vapour, although Oasis's climate had been described as 'tropical', so maybe that covered it.

He turned around and looked at the building he'd emerged from. It was monumentally ugly, like all architecture not built by religious devotees or reclusive eccentrics. Its only redeeming feature was the transparency of the mess hall's window, lit up like a video screen in the dark. Although he'd walked quite a long way, he could still recognise the coffee bar and the magazine rack, and even fancied he could make out the Asian man still slumped on one of the chairs. At this distance, these details looked like a neat assortment of items stored inside a coin-operated dispenser. A luminous little box, surrounded by a great sea of strange air; and, above it, a trillion miles of darkness.

He turned again and kept walking. His vague hope was that if he walked far enough, the featureless tarmac of the airport environs would finally come to an end, and he would step over into the landscape of Oasis, the real Oasis, the Oasis he had come to claim for the glory of God.

His denim jacket was growing heavy with moisture and his flannel shirt was swollen with perspiration. His jeans made a comical whooping noise as he walked, rough wet cotton rubbing against itself. The waistband was starting to chafe against his hips; a rivulet of sweat ran into the cleft of his arse. He stopped to hitch up his trousers and to wipe his face. He pressed his fingertips to his ears, to clear them of a sibilant undertone he'd been attributing to his sinuses. But the noise was not from within. The atmosphere was full of rustling. Wordless whispering, the sound of agitated leaves, except that there was no vegetation anywhere to be seen. It was as though the air currents, so similar to water currents, could not move silently, but must churn and hiss like ocean waves.

He was sure he'd adjust, in time. It would be like living near a railway line, or, indeed, near the ocean. After a while you wouldn't hear it any more.

He walked further, resisting an impulse to remove his clothes and toss them on the ground for retrieval on his return. The vista of tarmac showed no sign of ending. What could USIC possibly want with all this blank bitumen? Maybe there were plans to extend the accommodation wing, or build squash courts, or a shopping mall. Oasis was tipped, in 'the very near future', to become a 'thriving community'. By which USIC meant a thriving community of foreign settlers, of course. This world's indigenous inhabitants, thriving or otherwise, were scarcely mentioned in USIC's literature, except for fastidious assurances that nothing was planned or implemented without their full and informed consent. Let no one think for a moment that colonisation was on the agenda here; it wasn't even in the lexicon. USIC was 'in partnership' with the citizens of Oasis – whoever they might be.

Peter was certainly very much looking forward to meeting them. They were, after all, the whole reason he had come.

The Piano Man

JOANNA TROLLOPE (born Gloucestershire, 1943) studied at Oxford
and worked at the Foreign Office and in teaching before writing full
time. Awarded an OBE in 1986, she is the author of more than twenty
bestselling novels, including historical fiction under the name Caroline
Harvey. Her story for Ox-Tales is the opening chapter of a new novel, *The
Other Family*, to be published in 2010. Her younger daughter is currently
Oxfam's country director for Indonesia.

LOOKING BACK, IT ASTONISHED her that none of them had broken down in the hospital. Even Dilly, who could be relied on to burst into tears over a shed eyelash, had been completely mute. Chrissie supposed it was shock, literally, the sudden suspension of all natural reactions caused by trauma. And the trauma had actually begun before the consultant had even opened his mouth. They just knew, all four of them, from the way he looked at them, before he said a word. They knew he was going to say, 'I'm so very sorry, but—' and then he did say it. He said it all the way through to the end, and they all stared at him, Chrissie and the three girls. And nobody uttered a cheep.

Chrissie didn't know how she had got them home. Even though Tamsin and Dilly could drive, it hadn't crossed her mind to hand either of them the car keys. Instead, she had climbed wordlessly into the driver's seat, and Tamsin had got in – unchallenged, for once – beside her, and the two younger ones had slipped into the back and even put their seatbelts on without being reminded. Unheard of, usually. And Chrissie had started the car and driven them, upright behind the wheel as if she was trying to demonstrate good posture, up Highgate Hill and down the other side towards home, towards the house they had lived in since Amy was born, sixteen – nearly seventeen – years ago.

Of course, there was no parking space directly outside the house. There seldom was, in the evenings, after people got home from work.

Chrissie said, 'Oh bother,' in an over-controlled, lady-like way, and Dilly said, from the back seat, 'There's a space over there, outside the Nelsons,' and then nobody spoke while Chrissie manoeuvred the car in, very badly, because they were all thinking how he would have been, had he been there, how he would have said, 'Ornamental objects shouldn't be asked to do parking. Gimme the keys,' and Chrissie would – well, might, anyway – have laughed and thrown the keys at him ineptly, proving his point, and he'd have inserted the car neatly into an impossible space in no time so that they could all please him by saying, 'Show-off,' in chorus. 'I make my living from showing off,' he'd say. 'And don't you forget it.'

They got out of the car and locked it and trooped across the road to their own front door. There were no lights on.

It had been daylight when they left, and anyway, they were panicking because of the ambulance coming, and his frightening pallor and evident pain, so nobody thought of the return, how the return might be. Certainly, nobody had dared to think that the return might be like this.

Chrissie opened the front door, while the girls huddled behind her in the porch as if it was bitterly cold and they were desperate to get into the warmth. It occurred to Chrissie, irrelevantly, that she should have swept the leaves out of the porch, that it badly needed redecorating, that it had needed redecorating for years and Richie had always said that his granny, in North Shields on Tyneside, had scrubbed her front doorstep daily – except for Sundays – on her hands and knees. Daily. With a brush and a galvanised bucket.

Chrissie took the keys out of the door, and dropped them. Tamsin leaned over her mother's bent back and switched on the hall lights. Then they all pushed past and surged down the hall to the kitchen, and Chrissie straightened up, with the keys in her hand, and tried to put them into the door's inside lock and found she was shaking so badly that she had to hold her right wrist with her left hand, in order to be steady enough.

Then she walked down the hall, straight down, not looking in at the sitting room and certainly not in at his practise room, where the piano sat, and the dented piano stool, and

the framed photographs and the music system and the racks
and racks of CDs and the certificates and awards and battered stacks of old sheet music he would never throw away.
She paused in the kitchen doorway. All the lights were on
and so was the radio, at once, Kiss FM or something, and
the kettle was whining away and all three girls were scattered about, all separately, and they were all now crying and
crying.

Later that night, Chrissie climbed into bed clutching
a hot water bottle and a packet of Nurofen Extra. She
hadn't used a hot water bottle for years. She had an
electric blanket on her side of their great bed – Richie, a
Northerner, had despised electric blankets – but she had
felt a great need that night to have something to hold in
bed, something warm and tactile and simple, so she had
dug about in the airing cupboard and found a hot water
bottle that had once been given to Dilly, blue rubber inside a nylon fur cover fashioned to look like a Dalmatian,
its caricatured spotted face closing down over the stopper
in a padded mask.

One of the girls had put some tea by her bed. And a
tumbler of what turned out to be whisky. She never drank
whisky. Richie had liked whisky, but she always preferred

vodka. Or champagne. Richie would have made them drink champagne that evening; he always said champagne was grief medicine, temper medicine, disappointment medicine. But they couldn't do it. There was a bottle in the fridge – there was almost always a bottle in the fridge – and they took it out and looked at it and put it back again. They'd drunk tea, and more tea, and Amy had had some cereal, and Tamsin had gone to telephone her boyfriend – not very far away – and they could hear her saying the same things over and over again, and Dilly had tried to pick some dried blueberries out of Amy's cereal and Amy had slapped her and then Chrissie had broken down at last herself, utterly and totally, and shocked them all into another silence.

That shock, on top of the other unbearable shock, probably accounted for the whisky. And her bed being turned down, and the bedside lamp on, and the bathroom all lit and ready, with a towel on the stool. But there was still a second towel on the heated rail, the supersized towel he liked, and still six pillows on the bed, and his reading glasses were on top of the pile of books he never finished, and there were his slippers, and a half-drunk glass of water. Chrissie looked at the glass with a kind of terror. His mouth had been on that glass, last night. Last night only. And she was going to have to lie down beside it because nothing on earth could persuade her either to touch that glass or to let anyone else touch it.

'Mum?' Amy said from the doorway.

Chrissie turned. Amy was still dressed, in a mini dress and jeans and ballet slippers so shallow they were like a narrow black border to her naked feet. Chrissie said, gesturing at the bed, at the whisky, 'Thank you.'

'S'okay,' Amy said.

She had clamped some of her hair on top of her head with a red plastic clip and the rest hung unevenly round her face. Her face looked awful. Chrissie put her arms out.

'Come here.'

Amy came and stood awkwardly in Chrissie's embrace. It wasn't the right embrace, Chrissie knew; it wasn't relaxed enough, comforting enough. Richie had been the one who was good at comfort, at subduing resistant adolescent limbs and frames into affectionate acquiescence.

'Sorry,' Chrissie said, into Amy's hair.

Amy sighed.

'What for?' she said. 'You didn't kill him. He just died.'

For being here, Chrissie wanted to say, for being here when he isn't.

'We just have to do it,' she said instead, 'Hour by hour. We just have to get through.'

Amy shifted, half pulling away.

'I know.'

Chrissie looked at the Nurofen.

'Want something to relax you? Help you sleep.'

Amy grimaced. She shook her head. Chrissie said, 'What are the others doing?'

'Dilly's got her door shut. Tam's talking to Robbie.'

'*Still?*'

'Still,' Amy said. She looked round the bedroom. Her glance plainly hurried over the slippers, the far pillows. 'I don't know what to do.'

'Nor me,' Chrissie said.

Amy began to cry again. Chrissie tightened the arm round her shoulders, and pressed Amy's head against her.

'I know, baby—'

'I can't *stand* it—'

'Do you', Chrissie said, 'want to sleep with me?'

Amy stopped crying. She looked at the extra pillows. She shook her head, sniffing.

'Couldn't. Sorry.'

'Don't have to be sorry. Just a suggestion. We'll none of us sleep, wherever we are.'

'When I wake up next,' Amy said, 'there'll be a second, before I remember. Won't there?'

Chrissie nodded. Amy disengaged herself and trailed towards the door. In the doorway she paused and took the red clip out of her hair and snapped it once or twice.

'At least,' she said, not turning, not looking at her mother. 'At least we've got his name still. At least we're all still Rossiters.' She gave a huge shuddering sigh. 'I'm going to play my flute.'

'Yes,' Chrissie said, 'Yes. You do that.'

Amy flicked a glace at her mother.

'Dad liked my flute,' she said.

Then she went slowly away down the landing, shuffling in her little slippers, and Chrissie heard her starting tiredly on the stairs that led to the second floor conversion that she and Richie had decided on, and designed, so that Dilly and Amy could have bedrooms of their own.

She did sleep. She had thought she neither could, nor should, but she fell into a heavy, brief slumber and woke two hours later in order to fall, instead, into a pit of grief so deep that there seemed neither point nor possibility of climbing out of it. She had no idea how long she wrestled down there, but at some point she exchanged her embrace of the Dalmatian hot water bottle for one of Richie's pillows, scented with the stuff he used on the grey streaks in his hair, and found herself crushing it, and groaning, and being suddenly and simultaneously aware that there were lines of incipient daylight above the curtain tracks, and that a bird or two was tuning up in the plane tree outside the window. She rolled over and turned on the light. It was six thirteen. She was six hours and thirteen minutes, only, into the first day of this chapter of life which she had always dreaded and, consequently, had never permitted herself to picture.

'I'll be a hopeless widow,' she used to say to Richie, and, if he was paying attention, he'd say back, 'Well, I'm not giving you the chance to find out,' and then he'd sing her something, a line or two of some Tony Bennett or Jack Jones ballad, and deflect the moment. He'd always done that, defuse by singing. Once she had thought it was wonderful. Recently, however, in the last year or two, she thought he found it easier to sing than to engage. Oh God, if only! If only he *had* engaged! If only he'd done even that!

She drew her left hand out from under the duvet, and looked at it. It was a well-kept, pretty hand, as befitted a well-kept, pretty woman. It bore a narrow white gold plain band and a half-hoop of diamonds. The diamonds were quite big, bigger than they possibly might have been had they been dug out of the faraway depths of South Africa. Instead, they had been made, ingeniously, in a small factory near Antwerp, by a process which simulated what nature might have managed over millennia, but in only three weeks. They were, Chrissie told Richie, known as industrial diamonds. He had looked at her hand, and then his attention went back to his piano and he played a few bars of Gershwin, and then he said, 'You wear them, sweetheart. If they make you happy.'

She said, 'You know what would make me happy.'

Richie went on playing.

She said, 'I have to be Mrs Rossiter, for the girls. I have to be Mrs Rossiter at school. I have to wear a wedding ring and be Mrs Rossiter.'

'Okay,' Richie said softly. He began on some mounting chords. 'Course you do.'

'Richie—'

'Wear the rings,' Richie said. 'Wear them. Let me pay for them.'

But she hadn't. She told herself that it was principle, that a woman of independent mind could buy her own manifestations of the outward respectability required at the school gates, even in liberally minded North London. For a week or two, she registered the glances cast at her sizeable diamonds – and the conclusions visibly drawn in consequence – with satisfaction and even tiny flashes of triumph. But then heart quietly overcame head with its usual stealthy persistence, and the independence and the triumph faded before the miserable and energetic longing for her status as Mrs Rossiter to be a reality rather than a fantasy adorned with meaningless – and engineered – symbols.

It wasn't really just status, either. She was Richie's manager, after all, the controller and keeper of his diary, his finances, his pragmatically necessary well-being. She had plenty of status, in the eyes of Richie's profession, as Christine Kelsey, the woman – girl, back then – who had persuaded Richie Rossiter that a bigger, younger audience awaited him outside the Northern circuit where he had thus far spent all his performing life. Richie only answered the telephone for pleasure and left all administration, and certainly anything technological, to her. No, it wasn't really status, it really wasn't.

It was instead that hoary old, urgent old, irreplaceable old need for commitment. In twenty-three years together, Chrissie could not shift Richie one millimetre towards divorcing his wife, and marrying her. He wasn't Catholic, he wasn't in touch with his wife, he wasn't even much in touch with his son by that marriage. He was living in London, in apparent contentment, with a woman he had elected to leave his wife for, and the three daughters he had had by her and with whom he was plainly besotted, but he would make no move of any kind to transfer his legal position as head of his first family to his second.

For years, he said he would think about it, that he came from a place and a background where traditional codes of conduct were as fundamental to a person as their heartbeat, and therefore it would take him time. And Chrissie at first understood that and, a little later in this relationship, continued at least to try and understand it. But his efforts – such as they had ever really been – dwindled to invisibility over time, corresponding inevitably with a rise in Chrissie's anxiety and insistence. The more she asked – in a voice whose rigorously modulated control spoke volumes – the more he played his Gershwin. If she persisted, he switched to Rachmaninov, and played with his eyes closed. In the end – well, it now looked like the end – she had marched out and bought her industrial diamonds and, she now realised, surveying her left hand in the first dawn of her new widowhood, let him off the hook, by finding – as she so often did, good old Chrissie – a practical solution to living with his refusal.

She let her hand fall into the plumpness of the duvet. The girls were all Rossiter. Tamsin Rossiter, Delia Rossiter, Amy Rossiter. That was how they had all been registered at birth, with her agreement, encouragement even.

'It makes sense to have your name,' she'd said. 'After all, you're the well-known one. You're the one people will associate them with.'

She'd waited three times for him to say, 'Well, they're our children, pet, so I think you should join the Rossiter clan as well, don't you?', but he never did.

He accepted the girls as if it was entirely natural that they should be identified with him, and his pride and delight in them couldn't be faulted. Those friends from the North who had managed to accept Richie's transition to London and to Chrissie professed exaggerated amazement at his preparedness to share the chores of three babies in the space of five years: he was a traitor, they said loudly, glass in hand, jocular arm round Chrissie's shoulders, to the noble cause of unreconstructed Northern manhood. But none of them, however they might covertly stare at Chrissie's legs and breasts or overtly admire her cooking or her ability to get Richie gigs in legendarily impossible venues, ever urged him to marry her. Perhaps, Chrissie thought now, staring at the ceiling through which she hoped Dilly still slept, they thought he had.

After all, the girls did. Or, to put it another way, the girls had no reason to believe that he hadn't. They were all Rossiters, Chrissie signed herself Rossiter on all family concerned occasions, and they knew her professional name was Kelsey just as they knew she was their father's manager. It wouldn't have occurred to them that their parents weren't married, because the subject had simply never arisen. The disputes that arose between Richie and Chrissie were – it was the stuff of their family chronicle – because their father wanted to work less and play and sing more just for playing and singing's sake, and their mother, an acknowledged businesswoman, wanted to keep up the momentum. The girls, Chrissie knew, were inclined to side with their father. That was no surprise – he had traded, for decades, on getting women audiences to side with him. But – perhaps because of this, at least in part – the girls had found it hard to leave home. Tamsin and Dilly had both tried, and had come back again, and when they came home it was to their father that they had instinctively turned and it was their father who had made it plain that they were, literally, more than welcome.

Chrissie swallowed. She pictured Dilly, through that ceiling, asleep in her severe cotton pyjamas in the resolute order of her bedroom. Thank heavens, today, that she was there. And thank heavens for Amy, in her equally determined chaos in the next room, and for Tamsin amid the ribbons and flowers and china shoe collections down the landing. Thank heavens she hadn't prevailed, and achieved her aim of even attempted daughterly self-sufficiency before the girls reached the age of twenty. Richie had been right. He was wrong about a lot of things, but about his girls he had been right.

Chrissie began to cry again. She pulled her hand back in, under the duvet, and rolled on her side, where Richie's pillow awaited her in all its glorious, intimate, agonising familiarity.

'Where's Mum?' Tamsin said.

She was standing in the kitchen doorway clutching a pink cotton kimono round her as if her stomach hurt. Dilly was sitting at the table, staring out of the window in front of her, and the tabletop was littered with screwed-up balls of tissue. Amy was down the far end of the kitchen by the sink, standing on one leg, her raised foot in her hand, apparently gazing out into the garden. Neither moved.

'Where's Mum?' Tamsin said again.

'Dunno,' Dilly said.

Amy said, without turning, 'Did you look in her room?'

'Door's shut.'

Amy let her foot go.

'Well, then.'

Tamsin padded down the kitchen in her pink slippers.

'I couldn't sleep.'

'Nor me.'

She picked up the kettle and nudged Amy sideways so that she could fill it at the sink.

'I don't believe it's happened.'

'Nor me.'

'I can't—'

Cold water gushed into the kettle, bounced out and caught Amy's sleeve.

'Stupid cow!'

Tamsin took no notice. She carried the kettle back to its mooring.

'What are we gonna do?' Dilly said.

Tamsin switched the kettle on.

'Go back to the hospital. All the formalities—'

'How do you know?'

'It's what they said. Last night. They said it's too late now, but come back in the morning.'

'It's the morning now,' Amy said, still gazing into the garden.

Dilly half turned from the table.

'Will Mum know what to do?'

Tamsin took one mug out of a cupboard.

'Why should she?'

'Can I have some tea?' Amy said.

'What d'you mean, why should she?'

'Why should she', Tamsin said, her voice breaking, 'know what you do when your husband dies?'

Amy cried out, 'Don't say that!'

Tamsin got out a second mug. Then, after a pause, a third. She said, not looking at Amy, 'It's true, babe.'

'I don't want it to be!'

'None of us do,' Dilly said. She gathered all the tissue balls up in her hands and crushed them together. Then she stood up and crossed the kitchen and dumped them in the pedal bin. 'Is not being able to take it in worse than when you've taken it in?'

'It's all awful,' Amy said.

'Will Mum ..?' Dilly said, and stopped.

Tamsin was taking teabags out of a caddy their father had brought down from Newcastle, a battered tin caddy with a crude portrait of Earl Grey stamped on all four sides. The caddy had always been an object of mild family derision, being so cosy, so evidently much used, so sturdily unsleek. Richie had loved it. He said it was like one he had grown up with, in the terraced house of his childhood in North Shields. He said it was honest, and he liked it filled with Yorkshire teabags. Earl Grey tea – no disrespect to his lord- ship – was for toffs and for women.

Tamsin's hand shook now, opening it.

'Will Mum what?'

'Well,' Dilly said, 'Well, *manage*.'

Tamsin closed the caddy and shut it quickly away in its cupboard.

'She's very practical. She'll manage.'

'But there's the other stuff—'

Amy turned from the sink.

'Dad won't be singing.'

'No.'

'If Dad isn't singing—'

Tamsin poured boiling water into the mugs in a wavering steam.

'Maybe she can manage other people—'

'Who can?' Chrissie said from the doorway.

She was wearing Richie's navy blue bathrobe and she had pulled her hair back into a tight ponytail. Dilly got up from the table to hug her and Amy came running down the kitchen to join in.

'We were just wondering,' Tamsin said unsteadily.

Chrissie said into Dilly's shoulder, 'Me too.' She looked at Amy. 'Did anyone sleep?'

'Not really.'

'She played her flute,' Dilly said, between clenched teeth. 'She played and played her flute. I couldn't have slept even if I'd wanted to.'

'I didn't want to,' Tamsin said, 'because of having to wake up again.'

Chrissie said, 'Is that tea?'

'I'll make another one—'

Chrissie moved towards the table, still holding her daughters. They felt to her, at that moment, like the only support and sympathy that were of any use and at the same time like a burden of redoubled emotional intensity that she neither knew how to manage or to put down. She subsided into a chair, and Tamsin put a mug of tea in front of her. She glanced up.

'Thank you. Toast?'

'Couldn't,' Dilly said.

'Could you try? Just a slice? It would help; it really would.'

Dilly shook her head. Amy opened the larder cupboard and rummaged about in it for a while. Then she took out a packet of chocolate digestive biscuits and put them on the table.

'I'm trying', Dilly said tensely, 'not to eat chocolate.'

'You're a pain—'

'Sh,' Chrissie said. She took Dilly's nearest wrist. 'Sh. Sh.'

Dilly took her hand away and held it over her eyes.

'Dad ate those—'

'No, he didn't,' Amy said. 'No, he didn't. He ate those putrid ones with chocolate cream stuff in, he—'

'Please,' Chrissie said. She picked up her mug. 'What were you saying when I came in?'

Tamsin put the remaining mugs on the table. She looked at her sisters. They were looking at the table. She said, 'We were talking about you.'

Chrissie raised her head. 'And?' she said.

Tamsin sat down, pulling her kimono round her as if in the teeth of a gale.

Dilly took her hand away from her face. She said, 'It's just, well, will you – will we – be okay, will we manage, will we—'

There was a pause.

'I don't think', Chrissie said, 'that we'll be okay for quite a long time. Do you? I don't think we can expect to be. There's so much to get used to that we don't really want ... to get used to. Isn't there?' She stopped. She looked round the table. Amy had broken a biscuit into several pieces and was jigsawing them back together again. Chrissie said, 'But you know all that, don't you? You know all that as well as I do. You didn't mean that, did you – you didn't mean how are we going to manage emotionally, did you?'

'It seems', Tamsin said, 'so rubbish to even think of anything else ...'

'No,' Chrissie said. 'It's practical. We have to be practical. We have to live. We have to go on living. That's what Dad wanted. That's what Dad worked for.'

Amy began to cry quietly onto her broken biscuit.

Chrissie retrieved Dilly's hand and took Amy's nearest

one. She said, looking at Tamsin, gripping the others, 'We'll be fine. Don't worry. We have the house. And there's more. And I'll go on working. You aren't to worry. Anyway, it isn't today's problem. Today just has to be got through, however we can manage it.'

Tamsin was moving her tea mug round in little circles with her right hand and pressing her left into her stomach. She said, 'We ought to tell people.'

'Yes,' Chrissie said. 'We should. We must make a list.'

Tamsin looked up.

'I might be moving in with Robbie.'

Dilly gave a small scream.

'Not now, darling,' Chrissie said tiredly.

'But I—'

'Shut it!' Amy said suddenly.

Tamsin shrugged.

'I just thought if we were making plans, making lists—'

Amy leaned across the table. She hissed, 'We were going to make a list of who to tell that Dad died last night. Not lists of who we were planning to shack up with.'

Chrissie got up from the table.

'And the registrar,' she said. She began to shuffle through the pile of papers by the telephone. 'And the undertaker. And I suppose the newspapers. Always better to tell them than have them guess.'

Tamsin sat up straighter. She said, 'What about Margaret?'

Chrissie stopped shuffling.

'Who?'

'Margaret,' Tamsin said.

Amy and Dilly looked at her.

'Tam—'

'Well,' Tamsin said, 'she ought to be told. She's got a right to know.'

Amy turned to look across the kitchen at Chrissie. Chrissie was holding a notebook and an absurd pen with a plume of shocking pink marabou frothing out of the top.

'Mum?'

Chrissie nodded, slowly.

'I know—'

'But Dad wouldn't want that!' Dilly said. 'Dad never spoke to her, right? She wasn't part of his life, was she? He wouldn't have wanted her to be part of – of ...' She stopped. Then she said, angrily, 'It's nothing to do with her.'

Amy stood up and drifted down the kitchen again. Chrissie watched her, dark hair down her back, Richie's dark hair, Richie's dark Northern hair, only girl version.

'Amy?'

Amy didn't turn.

'I shouldn't have mentioned her,' Tamsin said. 'I shouldn't. She's no part of this.'

'I hate her,' Dilly said.

Chrissie said, making an effort, 'You shouldn't. She couldn't help being part of his life before and she's never made any claim, any trouble.'

'But she's *there*,' Dilly said.

'And', Amy said from the other end of the kitchen, 'she was his wife.'

'*Was*,' Tamsin said.

Chrissie held the notebook and the feathered pen hard against her. She said, 'I'm not sure I can quite ring her.'

'Nor me,' Dilly said.

Tamsin took a tiny mobile phone out of her kimono pocket and put it on the table.

'You can't really just *text* her.'

Chrissie made a sudden little fluttering gesture with the hand not holding the notebook. She said, 'I don't think I can quite do this, I can't manage ...' She stopped, and put her hand over her mouth.

Tamsin jumped up.

'Mum—'

'I'm okay,' Chrissie said, 'really I am. I'm fine. But I know you're right. I know we should tell Margaret.'

'And Scott,' Amy said.

Chrissie glanced at her.

'Of course. Scott. I forgot him, I forgot—'

Tamsin moved to put her arms round her mother.

'Damn,' Chrissie whispered against Tamsin. 'Damn. I don't—'

'You don't have to,' Tamsin said.

'I do. I do. I do have to tell Margaret and Scott that Dad has died.'

Nobody said anything. Dilly got up and collected the mugs on the table and put them in the dishwasher. Then she swept the biscuit crumbs and bits into her hand and put them in the bin, and the remaining packet in the cupboard. They watched her, all of them. They were used to watching Dilly, so orderly in her person and her habits, so chaotic in her reactions and responses. They waited while she found a cloth, wiped the table with it, rinsed it and hung it, neatly folded, over the mixer tap on the sink.

Chrissie said, absently, approvingly, 'Thank you, darling.'

Dilly said, furiously, 'It doesn't matter if bloody Margaret knows!'

Chrissie sighed. She withdrew a little from Tamsin.

'It does matter.'

'Dad wouldn't want it!'

'He would.'

'Well, do it then!' Dilly shouted.

Chrissie gave a little shiver.

'I'd give anything—'

'I'll stand beside you', Tamsin said, 'while you ring.'

Chrissie gave her a small smile.

'Thank you.'

'Mum?'

Chrissie turned. Amy was leaning against the cupboard where the biscuits lived. She had her arms folded.

'Yes, darling.'

'I'll do it.'

'What?'

'I'll ring her,' Amy said. 'I'll ring Margaret.'

Chrissie put her arms out.

'You're lovely. You're a doll. But you don't have to. You don't know her—'

Amy shifted slightly.

'Makes it easier, then, doesn't it?'

'But—'

'Look,' Amy said, 'I don't mind phones. I'm not scared of phones, me. I'll just dial her number and tell her who I am and what's happened and then I'll say goodbye.'

'What if she wants to come to the funeral?' Dilly said. 'What if she wants to come and make out he was ...?'

'Shut up,' Tamsin said.

She looked at her mother.

'Let her,' Tamsin said. 'Let her ring.'

'Really?'

'Yes,' Tamsin said. 'Let her do it like she said and then it'll be done. Two minutes and it'll be done.'

'And then?'

'There won't be an "and then".'

Amy peeled herself off the cupboard and stood up. She looked as she looked, Chrissie remembered, when she learned to dive, standing on the end of the springboard, full of excited, anxious tension. She winked at her mother, and she actually smiled.

'Watch me,' Amy said.

(One Last) Throw
of the Dice

GILES FODEN (born Warwickshire, 1967) grew up in Malawi. Between 1990 and 2006 he worked as a journalist on the *TLS* and the *Guardian*. In 2007 he was appointed Professor of Creative Writing at the University of East Anglia. His first three novels all have African settings: *The Last King of Scotland* (1998; a Whitbread First Novel winner and subsequently a major film) takes place during Idi Amin's rule of Uganda in the 1970s; *Ladysmith* (1999) is set in the Anglo-Boer War in 1899; and *Zanzibar* (2002) explores East Africa in 1998, amid the bombings of American embassies. His latest novel, *Turbulence* (2009), shifts to the D-Day Normandy landings; '(One Last) Throw of the Dice' is an alternative ending to that book.

SCHLOMBORG KNOCKS ON THE DOOR of my cabin, making unfriendly noises about my forecast for the next twelve hours. 'Typhoon you say coming?' he says, poking his reddish, Edward VII beard round the door. 'Tyfon' is how he pronounces it, in his natural Swedish.

'It isn't so bad, is it?' he continues, hopefully.

'I am afraid it is,' I say. 'Pressure is falling, temperature is rising.'

'Your last forecast was not very right.'

'That may be so,' I say, 'but there is a typhoon on the way, nonetheless. It might involve a whirlpool. You should order the lifeboats be readied.'

He waits, as if expecting something supplementary, before withdrawing his kingly phiz. Ever since I went AWOL in Dar, he had begun to doubt me. Once he has gone, I wonder what it is going to be like – to be in the eye of the storm, where all learning counts for nothing.

Later in the day, the first signs of the typhoon begin to appear on the horizon. It is as if someone has thrown effervescent black dye into the sky. I join Schlomborg on the bridge watching these distant black stirrings. They are like worms trying to form themselves into letters. Schlomborg wants to know why an electronic early-warning device he's had installed did not give notice of the coming storm.

'A system like that', I tell my affronted critic, 'will get nowhere near interpreting the weather properly. It wouldn't have a snowball's chance in hell.'

'A snowball's chance in hell.' In his strong accent, Schlomborg slowly repeats my words. 'Why do you say that? What is the object of talking like that?'

As the sonar plinks behind us, we look out of the wide window of the bridge. There will be a whirlpool. Far away, foam streaks are converging, pulling around a central point in gyratory fashion. The chasm will soon be within sight: a belt of deepening foam, organising itself into a broad-mouthed, yet tight-knitted cone – into whose desperate declivity the *Habbakuk* is even now being inevitably drawn by a complex force of circulation.

Stretching across the whole horizon like a theatrical backdrop, the storm is too big to sail round; the only thing to do is sail into it. So Schlomborg sets the course and we continue on the deep – cutting through the open main to a doom unknown. As we sail on – we're somewhere near

Djibouti – the temperature increases, as expected. I fear for the integrity of the ship. It seems impossible that our cargo of super-frozen water will ever reach the desert.

My mind whirs. The separate incidents of the early part of the voyage become melded together in my head like slabs of Pykerete, that curious mixture of ice and wood pulp from which our vessel is made. The falcon belonging to Saïd freezing and falling off his perch (we revived it with a hairdryer); the Sheikh (Saïd's father and the ship's owner) sitting cross-legged in his zebra-skin slippers; the enjoyable backgammon games I played with Saïd, laughing at the dice.

As the storm grows closer (how impotent is man in the face of such phenomena), I reflect on the hurried accidents of my life, which have caused me to focus on a search for an underlying plan. I have been hoping that it would emerge, on this last voyage, from the prevailing drift. Like a net in water. A fishing net drawn taut and lifted out of the ocean ... But it was never going to happen that way. All that search for order was wrong-headed. I created a false adversary: weather in my head. Now it has become material. The barometer has been falling with every mile, the temperature rapidly rising. In a matter of hours, the typhoon could be here. I have done what I can. The only thing to do now is eat.

I say to Saïd in the lunch queue, 'I think we are in for a violent tropical storm.'

He says, 'Yes, it is becoming almost as hot as my own country. It would make even a holy man quarrelsome.' He is a tall, handsome boy with an aquiline nose and tightly curled hair. The contrast between the undulating blackness of his beard and bits of rice that have stuck in it, when that happens, is startling.

After lunch we go outside to watch an ominous sky- and seascape. Saïd collects his falcon on the way. The deck is almost clear, except for the conning tower and other parts of the superstructure of the bridge. Saïd stands next to me at the taffrail, yearning, I suppose, for conversation. But we don't speak for a while, simply watch instead the water grow, Saïd every now and then stroking the neck of the falcon.

'How far', he says eventually, 'does this swell come from?'

'It's misleading to think of each wave as a separate unit,' I reply. 'It is the whole that counts. Waves are an effect propagated through a unified mass of water. Much of human affairs is like that. What are in fact waves we see as particles. But this weather, yes, it looks like it has come from far away.'

'It will calm, yes?'

'A change in the weather can pacify even the most powerful waves – but I think this storm will be very powerful indeed, not likely to change its identity easily.'

The falcon shifts on the glove. It gazes out over the roughening sea. At waves hitting the hull, or curling out sideways under the black-streaked orange glow of the sun: the bird's merciless eye squaring up to the implacability of the ocean.

'So much salt,' Saïd says, as the white-capped water slides away beneath us. 'There is something sad about the sea.'

'And angry,' I add, gripping the taffrail. The waves are getting higher, tearing away at the hull as if the idea of a ship made of ice is an abomination. As if to confirm this, the *Habbakuk* suddenly plunges forward, like a stumbling horse.

'It will be all right?' asks Saïd, anxiously.

I suddenly see an abyssal future. 'I don't know, to be honest. I am no longer confident in the ship's structure. The melting calculations I have done do not take into account storms above average violence. You may think that strange, with me being a forecaster, but there were too many variables.'

Saïd – sweet, companionable Saïd – is quiet for a moment. Then he says: 'Maybe I will become a weather forecaster. Tell me, what ... language is best for telling somebody a forecast of the weather? I mean words and phrases, not Arabic or French or English. When you did D-Day how did you speak to the commander-in-chief? How did you make the forecast come true in his mind?'

I think about this for a while before replying. 'I didn't speak to the commander-in-chief. Or the Supreme Commander, as we called him. That was another man. But, as to your question, it is not simply a matter of words and phrases. It comes slowly. It comes by being yourself and by working visibly near the people who desire the forecast. You get nowhere if you are not open, if you don't let them see what you are doing. You just have to be good and show that you are good, without intruding on the speciality of the person you have to persuade. No gimmicks, no glossing over. You have to avoid obscurity and any type of ambiguity, saying nothing you believe to be false or for which you lack evidence. You must be brief, orderly and specific, giving as much information as required, but no more.'

As I speak, I think of my own relationship with Schlomborg. The falcon rears on Saïd's wrist, making his leather-clad hand rise as if pulled by a string from the sky.

'Are you going to let it fly?' I ask.

'Yes,' says the Sheikh's son. 'But I must feed him quickly, or else he will keep flying and flying until he sees land. Most likely he would exhaust himself.'

He releases the bird from its chain. It hoiks itself into the air, seems to hover for a moment, then sets out swiftly, like an arrow from a string. In this manner it tears off down the wooden-sheathed deck, before wheeling back, dipping under the taffrail. We watch it come back, halfway between us and the darkening, disappearing water before flashing up close to our faces.

Again and again the encirclement is made, in a progressively narrowing gyre – until Saïd, who has taken something out of his jacket pocket, spins round himself and throws his hand up in the air. Whereupon the falcon swoops and is gone. Then I realise he's on the roof of the bridge, where we can see Schlomborg glaring at us through the windows, surrounded by a glow of radar screens. With no less sullen an air, the bird is holding something in its claw, ripping at it with its beak in rhythmic movements.

'What was that you threw?' I ask.

At once Saïd slips his hand into his pocket again and – it is like a conjuring trick – what comes out, its head protruding from his clutched fist, is a custard-yellow chick.

'My God,' I say. 'I'd no idea.'

'That is the problem with you Europeans and Americans,' says Saïd in a friendly tone, holding up the chick for the falcon to see. 'You have forgotten to remember that you have no idea. You have forgotten that God's ways are not our ways. You think you can just bull ahead and God has nothing to do with it. Whereas the truth is that all the models we put on the world fail to measure up to his greatness.'

'I am an atheist these days,' I say stonily, irritated by this sudden onset of criticism.

The prince – for as the son of the Sheikh he is indeed a prince – flings the chick up into the air and once again the falcon is over us, come like an angel from some vast, unsearchable reach of another atmosphere.

We watch him return to the roost with his prey. 'You can't fool me, Professor Meadows,' says Saïd. 'I think in reality you are a spiritual man.'

'I was a Catholic once.' Then, anxious to change the subject, 'Where do you get those chicks?'

'Come,' says Saïd.

I follow him along the companionway to one of the sets of steps which lead down into the bowels of the ice ship. It is much colder down here and the air is full of the sound of the nacelles. It is a beautiful, if slightly disturbing sound, not at all like the grinding or chugging one usually hears in ships. Anyway, this is what fills my ears as I follow Saïd down a long, slightly damp passageway, its Pykerete walls lit with striplights. The only other noise is the murmuring of the Baluchis, some of whose cabins we pass, their doors curtained with straw mats or pieces of dyed cloth.

We walk on, into the very bottom of the ship. Then Saïd suddenly turns off right, opening a door into a room I do not know about, or have forgotten the existence of. A blast of heat and light dunts me in the face and I see to my astonishment that there is a large wooden ring in the room, a circular pen, over which three large aluminium lights are suspended and in the midst of which stands a large electric blow-heater. Around this mill hundreds of small yellow chicks, cheeping away for all they are worth. It makes me think of Brownian motion, or the manifestation of some other vital force at the heart of the universe. 'Goodness,' I say. 'I had no idea this was here. I thought I knew everything about this vessel.'

'That is what I mean,' says Saïd, his white teeth gleaming. 'You think you are a prophet, yet part of it you cannot know.'

The sound made by the chicks increases in volume as Saïd approaches a burlap sack of maize, which is leaning in a corner, its flap of brown casually half-folded over the golden corn.

'I see,' I say, watching Saïd throw them some, which they leap on eagerly. 'You keep them alive for a while, but you know they are going to die in the end.'

He puts the little shovel with which he has thrown the corn back on top of the burlap sack. 'It is Allah's will.'

'Maybe,' I say. 'But – you can't have all this heat down here! It's not in my calculations!'

'We will address ourselves to the individual in charge.'

'I presume you mean your father? You don't understand. It's unforeseen warming. Unforeseen concentrated calefaction!'

'Concentrated calefaction?' I see that he is smiling.

'The heater, the points of the light beams ... Never mind. A technical issue.' I am filled with anxiety, but with the typhoon coming there hardly seems any point in explaining.

I feel as if I am being whirled round at the centre of the universe – a universe which is itself being whirled round in the orbit of another, and another, and another – each one cut off from the secret withheld like a corpse by its arm.

I look at the three lamps pumping down on the little yellow chicks, who seem like the inhabitants of some science-fiction world. My gaze moves to Saïd, who is leaning over the rim of the circular wooden pen, still smiling. 'You don't get it, do you? When I see this, Saïd, I'm so shocked I have to ask myself how it can exist. This arrangement of yours could burn a hole in the freeboard.'

As if to confirm my anxieties, a piece of Pykerete as big as the palm of my hand falls from the panel above the lights, banging on one of the aluminium shades as if it were a gong, before tumbling into the pen below. Falling over themselves in a paroxysm of predatory pecking, the chicks set upon it.

We return to our cabins, almost being knocked over by the wind as we walk, grabbing from pillar to post, doused by water surging above the taffrail. I wonder why Schlomborg has not yet issued the order that the lifeboats be readied.

Even back inside, soaked, the surf seems to howl within. I wait. And then it comes: the frenzied vortex I predicted. The ship begins to tip. I look out of the porthole. I have heard of giant whirlpools, but this is a meteorological wonder. Unbelievable. Fantastic. Also deadly.

Now, surely, we are in the maelstrom itself – in the gaping, whirling trough, listing from side to side, all the surges of water smoothing round us as an enormous force begins to suck down.

The Baluchis are letting out strange cries, utterances of woe, their voices shrill and faint according to the rotation and their relative position. I feel a paralysis of terror, then steel myself to face it – to go and find out why Schlomborg has not readied the boats.

I find the Swede sitting cross-legged on the floor, his cap in his hand. 'Vot you vant?' he says to me savagely, his face covered with peculiar specks of lights – strange reflections from the directional lights of the nacelle controls.

Some direction! Helpless, whirled in irresistible revolutions, we are starting to fall. Water is boiling up by the conning window. There is not much time.

Schlomborg lies down on his side like a pig and covers his face with his hands. I am appalled that someone can abandon all sense of duty so precipitately.

'The boats – the boats – you must get them all to the boats.' I lean down and grab him by the lapels of his jacket. 'Come on! You must get them to the boats.'

Pulled up, plump in his uniform, he looks at me with an expression that is half-scorn, half-fear. I realise he has already given up; he just touches his red beard and lets his head hang. Then he says, 'Dese cattle do not deserve to be saved.'

GILES FODEN

I want to hit him and ... I do. He receives my blows with equanimity, simply holding up his hands on either side of his ears. As I am cuffing him, the ship moves violently. I lose my footing and trip – there is all sorts of stuff sliding to and fro on the floor of the bridge, including books, pieces of clothing and the walkie-talkies of the Arab first officers, who have either fled or are trying to get the boats out. Disoriented, I feel myself fall over as the ship angles even more. Somehow my limbs and Schlomborg's become mixed up and we roll like a pair of pub brawlers into a corner of the bridge. Two tins of foie gras fall with us and also those velvet, oversize dice with which Saïd and I had played backgammon, for want of the proper ones.

Then the *Habbakuk* itself slips violently in the other direction and we follow it. As we tumble, one of the tins of foie gras bounces off my forehead. I catch a cockeyed glimpse of a chart pinned up on the wall.

'Oh no,' gasps Schlomborg. 'Not zat.'

Landing on him in the other corner – we are face to face – I see his frightened eyes commanded by something behind me which, twisting, I perceive to be the conning window in the process of being broken through by a great volume of water ... that proceeds to fling me out of the bridge, spluttering down the metal stairs and onto the deck.

I can hardly hear my own voice as I call, slithering into

the seething mass of foam that has taken the *Habbakuk* in its grip. 'Lifeboats! For your lives!' I shout, utterly in vain, so loud is the noise of rushing water.

The deck is at an angle of fifteen degrees and to stop myself slipping I have to grab onto a steel ladder fixed on the wall. Pieces of pykerete are flying past, broken off by the force of the whirlpool. Seeing the Sheikh knocked down, taking a header into the base of a stanchion, I realise I will have to lash myself down if I am not to meet the same fate. There is a coil of line hanging from a post on the other side of the deck, so yelling like a madman I launch myself across the mountain of sea and, more by luck than judgement, catch hold of the rope on the other side.

The storm seems to subside a little, as does the sensation of falling into a pit. I become aware I have cut my thigh somehow, gouged out some flesh so there is actually a hole there. Tying myself to the taffrail with one end of the rope, I see a confused, writhing crowd of Baluchis pass down the deck. They are wading through the waves, which are now waist-high. They go out of view, then suddenly are there again, swept back by a brutal bar of water, raised once more to its previous level of intensity. Each time they pass, they are followed by some of their belongings – bags and parcels, boxes bound with string, cloth bundles – all kspringing out of the hold in crazy heaps and sliding along the deck.

Three times I feel the giant whirlpool spin us round, three times I see some of those poor men flung off. On the third time the maelstrom lifts the stern aloft and plunges the prow below, breaking – with a cataclysmic sound – the *Habbakuk* in two places in the middle. The Pykerete splinters like glass, bursting out of its wooden casing.

I see that the prow part is already deep in the treacherous funnel of the whirlpool and watch horrified from my lashed point in the middle as the stern quivers in the air and then – oh, God! goes down round and round to join its brother.

A small crowd of us are gathered in the middle, clasping whatever we can. We are utterly helpless in the rush of water: it is like a croupier is raking us to and fro. With two ends of the ship gone, the chance we will all go off the side is almost a certainty. If only I can get the rope across the deck somehow, then we will have something to hold on to . . .

With my lungs already half full of water, the idea of swimming seems horrible. Then I see Saïd, water coursing down him, both arms grasping a bollard. What goes through my mind, oddly and improbably, are the velvet dice and the games of backgammon we used to play. Is it worth, at this stage, making one last throw? Securing his attention with a sharp cry, I undo my rope from the taffrail – the rope whose other end is tied round my waist – and launch it through the air towards him.

Look at Me,
I Need a Smile

MICHAEL MORPURGO (born St Albans, 1943) taught for ten years before setting up, with his wife Clare, Farms for City Children, which each year invites over 3000 children a year to come and live on a working farm for a week of muck and magic! He is the author of more than 120 books for young people, many of which tackle the great issues of our age. Among the most popular are *War Horse* (1984), currently a National Theatre production in the West End, *Why the Whales Came* (1985), which was made into a film starring Helen Mirren and Paul Schofield, *Kensuke's Kingdom* (1999) which won the Children's Book Award, and *Private Peaceful* (2003) which won the Blue Peter award. In 2003 Michael became the Children's Laureate and in 2006 he was awarded an OBE. 'Look at Me I Need a Smile' is an extract from his latest book, *Running Wild* (2009).

THE YOUNG MAHOUT who was leading the elephant, some-times by the ear, sometimes by the trunk, was wearing a long white shirt that flapped loosely about him. The elephant kept trying to curl his trunk around it, tugging at it. The mahout ignored him and walked on, speaking all the while to the elephant in confidential whispers. I longed to know what he was saying, but didn't dare ask. He looked friendly enough, smiling at me whenever he glanced back up at me to see if I was all right. But he didn't seem to want to talk, and anyway I wasn't sure he spoke any English. But I knew that if we didn't get talking, then I'd be left alone again with my thoughts, and I didn't want that. And besides, I really wanted to find out more about this elephant I was riding. I decided to risk it and talk.

'What's he called?' I asked him.

'This elephant is not he. He is she,' he told me, in near perfect English. 'Oona. She is called Oona if you want to know. She is twelve years old, and she is like a sister to me. I know her from the first day she is born.'

Once the young man had started talking, he didn't seem to want to stop. He spoke very fast, too fast, and never once turned round, so he wasn't at all easy to understand. I had to listen hard. He went on, trying all the while to extricate his shirt tail from the grip of the elephant's trunk. 'This elephant, she likes this shirt very much, and she also likes people. Oona is very friendly, very intelligent too, and naughty. She is very naughty sometimes, you would not believe it. Sometimes she wants to run when I do not want her to run, and once she is running she is very hard to stop. Then once she is stopped, she is very difficult to start again. You know what Oona likes best? I tell you. She likes the sea. But it is a strange thing. Not today. Today she does not like the sea. I think maybe she is not feeling so good today. I take her down to the sea early this morning for her swim like I always do, and she does not want to go in. She does not want to go near. She only stands there looking out to sea as if she never saw it before. I tell her that the sea is the same as it was yesterday, but still she will not go in. One thing I know for sure: you can't make Oona do what Oona does not want to do.'

He tugged his shirt free at last. 'Thank you, Oona, very nice of you,' he said, stroking her ear. 'You see, she is happier now, and I think maybe this is because she likes you.

I can tell this when I look in her eyes. It is how elephants speak, with their eyes. This is a true thing.'

I did not ask any more questions after that, because I was far too busy just enjoying myself. I was savouring every moment of this ride. The elephant, I noticed then, was strangely mottled, with a sort of pink pigmentation under her grey skin. A pink elephant! I laughed out loud, and the elephant tossed her trunk as if she understood the joke and didn't much like it.

Everything I was seeing was new and exciting to me, the deep blue of the waveless ocean on one side, the shadowy green of the jungle on the other, where the trees came down to the sand. And beyond the trees I could see the hills climbing higher and higher into the far distance until they disappeared into clouds. Ahead of me the narrow strand of white beach seemed to go on for ever. I was hoping my ride would go on for ever too. I was thinking that maybe Mum had been right, that this was the perfect place to forget. But I didn't forget. I couldn't.

Mum and I had drifted through the days like sleepwalkers, enduring it all together, the phonecalls, the cards, the dozens of bunches of flowers left outside their door. The television news kept showing the same photograph of Dad, always in his uniform, never as he was at home.

Then there was the silent drive to the airport with

Grandpa and Grandma in the front. Beside me in the back seat, Mum looked steadfastly out the window all the way. But she did squeeze my hand from time to time, to reassure me, and I would do the same in return. It became a secret sign between us, a kind of confidential code. One squeeze meant, 'I'm here. We'll get through this together.' Two meant, 'Look at me. I need a smile.'

Out on the tarmac of the windswept airfield, we stood and watched the plane land, and taxi to a standstill. A piper was playing, as the flag-covered coffin was borne out from inside the plane, slowly, slowly, by soldiers from Dad's regiment. After, there were more long days of silent sadness, with Grandma and Grandpa still staying on in the house and doing everything for us, Grandma cooking meals we didn't want to eat, Grandpa out in the garden trimming the hedges, mowing the lawn, weeding the flower bed, Grandma busying herself endlessly around the house, cleaning, tidying, polishing, ironing. There were telephone calls to answer, and the doorbell too. A lot of callers had to be kept at bay. Grandpa did that. There was the shopping to do as well. He did that too. Sometimes we did it together, and I liked that. It got me out of the house.

For the funeral, people lined the streets and the church was packed. A piper played a lament over the graveside in the rain, and soldiers fired a volley into the air. The echoes of it seemed to go on for ever. Afterwards, as they walked away, I saw that everyone was holding onto their hats in the wind, except for the soldiers, whose berets seemed to stay on somehow, and I wondered how they did that. Whenever I looked up I found people staring at me. Were they looking to see if I was crying? Well, I wouldn't, not so long as Mum was there beside me squeezing my hand, once, twice.

At the gathering of family and friends in the house afterwards, everyone seemed to be speaking in hushed voices over their teacups. I was longing for it to be over. I wanted them all to go. I wanted only to be left alone in the house with Mum. Grandpa and Grandma were the last to go. They'd been wonderful, I knew they had, but I could see Mum was as relieved as I was when at last we said our goodbyes to them later that evening. We stood by our front gate and watched them drive away. Two hand-squeezes and a smile. It was over.

But it wasn't. Dad's fishing coat hung in the hallway, his Chelsea scarf around its shoulders. His boots were by the back door, still muddy from the last walk we'd all had together along the river to the pub. He'd bought me a packet of cheese and onion crisps that day, and there'd been a bit of an argument about that, because Mum had found the empty crisp packet in my anorak pocket afterwards – she always hated me eating that kind of food.

Whenever we went up to town to Stamford Bridge to see Chelsea play, Dad and I always had a pie and some crisps at the same pub, out in the street if it was fine weather, and everyone would be wearing blue. We'd walk to the ground afterwards. The whole street was a river of blue, and we were part of the river. I liked the ritual of getting to the match as much as the game itself. Sooner or later, after we got back home, Mum would always ask what we'd had for lunch, and we would always tell her, confess it sheepishly, and she would tell us both off. I loved it when we were both told off together – it was all part of it, of going to the football with Dad.

Dad's fishing rod was standing there in the corner by the deep freeze where it always was, and his ukulele lay where he'd left it on top of the piano. Beside it, there was the photo of Dad, smiling out at me, proudly holding up the ten-pound pike he'd caught. Often, when Dad was away, on exercise somewhere or overseas – and recently he had been away a lot – I would reach out, and touch the photo. Sometimes when I was quite sure no one else was around, I'd even talk to him, and tell him my troubles. The photo had always been like a treasured icon to me, a talisman. But now I tried all I could to avoid looking at it at all because I knew it would only make me feel sad again if I did. I felt bad about that, but I preferred to feel bad than sad. I was so filled up with sadness that there was no room for any more.

Some days I would wake up in the morning thinking and believing it had all been a nightmare, that Dad would be having his breakfast in the kitchen as usual when I got downstairs, that he'd be walking me to school as usual. Then I'd remember, and I'd know it was no nightmare, no dream, that the worst really had happened.

I was back at school a week or so after the funeral. Everyone was kind, too kind. I could tell that no one really wanted to talk to me. Even Charlie and Tonk and Bart, my best friends – they had been all my life – even they were keeping their distance. They didn't seem to know what to say to me. Nothing was how it had been. Everything and everyone was suddenly awkward. The teachers were all being sugary kind; Mr Mackenzie too, the headteacher – 'Big Mac' we all called him. He was sweetness itself, and that wasn't natural. No one was natural any more. Everyone was pretending. It made me feel alone, as if I didn't belong there any more.

One morning, I decided I just couldn't stand it. I put my hand up in class, and asked if I could go to the toilet. But I didn't go to the toilet. I just walked out of the school, and went home. Mum wasn't there and the house was locked. I sat on the doorstep and waited for her. That's where Big Mac found me when he came looking for me. Even then he wasn't cross. Mum was called away from her work at the hospital. She was upset, I could see that, and told me how worried everyone had been, but she wasn't angry with me either. I was almost hoping she would be. It wasn't the only time I ran away.

One afternoon Mum met me at the school gates in her nurse's uniform. I usually walked home on my own after school, so I knew something was up. She had news, she said, good news. Grandma had come to stay with us again, and without Grandpa this time. I wasn't at all happy about that. I was even less happy when Grandma kept telling me at teatime that I should eat up my toast 'like a good boy'. That was when Mum told me.

'We've been thinking, Grandma and me, we've been talking it over, Will,' she began. 'And we've decided that you need more time to settle down, that maybe I sent you back to school too soon, that maybe we've rushed back into things too quickly, both of us, I mean. People have been really kind, and really considerate. Mr Mackenzie at school agreed at once, so did the hospital. They all think we should go away for a while. They've said that we can take as long as we like, and to come back only when we're really ready to.'

This all sounded more than fine to me, but when Grandma interrupted it got even better, because that was when Grandma told me that she'd worked it all out, that we would be coming down to stay on the farm for a month or so. 'I've told your mum, Will,' she went on. 'I said I won't take no for an answer. You'll be staying for Christmas, and for as long as you like afterwards, for as long as it takes.' Mum and I exchanged a look and a smile at that, because Grandma never took no for an answer anyway.

'Grandma thinks it'll be a really good break for both of us, just what we need,' Mum told me. 'What do you think, Will?'

'All right,' I said, with a shrug. But I was over the moon.

Every day of our stay had been brilliant, except, that is, for a surprise visit to the doctor for some sort of injection that Mum said was important. 'All kids have it at your age,' she explained. I protested, but I could see I was getting nowhere. In the doctor's surgery, I looked the other way as the needle went in, but it still hurt like hell. But that apart, and despite Grandma being her usual bossy self, I'd had the best of times.

So it had come as a complete surprise to me when Mum suddenly announced we wouldn't be staying on with Grandma and Grandpa for Christmas, after all, but that the suitcases were already packed and we'd be going home by train that morning. Grandma was going to drive us to the station.

When the train got in, we took a taxi home, which I thought was a bit odd, because Mum had always made out that taxis were a waste of money, and far too expensive. As the taxi stopped outside home, she turned to me and told me to stay where I was, that she wouldn't be long. She asked the driver if he'd mind waiting a minute or two. She seemed suddenly excited, almost as if she were trying to suppress a giggle.

'Where are you going, Mum?' I asked her, but she was out of the taxi by now and running up the path into the house. She didn't answer me. I couldn't make head or tail of what was going on.

It wasn't long before she was out again carrying a heavy suitcase. 'Can you take us back to the station, please?' she asked the driver.

'Take you to the moon, if you're paying, darling,' he said.

'Not going to the moon, not quite that far,' Mum told him, breathlessly, as she climbed back into the taxi.

Then she told me to close my eyes. When I opened them again, she was flourishing two passports at me, a huge smile on her face. 'Grandma's idea,' she said, 'and I promise you, Will, it's the best idea she ever had – actually, I think it was Grandpa's. Anyway, she said that they thought it would be good for us to have Christmas away on our own, just the two of us, somewhere very special, somewhere we can forget … y'know, somewhere thousands of miles away.'

She took a brochure out of her bag, and waved that at me too. 'Look, Will! There's the hotel. There's the beach. There's the sea and the sand. And do you know where that is? Indonesia, where my family come from. I've never ever been there, and now I'm going, and you're coming with me. Full of surprises, your grandma. She never asked. Well, she wouldn't, would she? She just went ahead and booked it. "A Christmas present from Grandpa and me," she says. "You just go and enjoy yourselves." Mum's whole face was bright with laughter now. 'All we needed were those injections – remember, Will? – then just our passports, our summer things, and we're on our way.'

'What, now? We're going now?'

'Right now.'

'What about school?'

'No more school, not for the time being. Don't worry, I've asked Mr Mackenzie. He's fine about it. We're going to chill, Will.'

It was one of Dad's old jokes. This was the first time we'd really laughed in a very long time. It turned to tears soon enough. Crying together, I discovered then, was so much better than crying alone. We clung to one another in the back of the taxi, and at last began to let go of our grief.

At the station, the taxi driver helped us out with the suitcases. He wouldn't accept any payment. 'It's on me,' he said, taking Mum by the hand, and helping her out. 'It took me a while to work out who you were. I was in the crowd outside the church at the funeral. I saw you and the lad. I was a soldier once myself. In the Falklands. A while ago, but you don't forget. Lost my best friend out there. You have a good holiday now. I reckon you deserve it.'

I'd been on a plane a few times before, to Switzerland. But this plane was massive. It took an age lumbering down the runway before it lifted off. There was a moment when I thought it never would. I had my own screen, so that I could choose whatever film I wanted. I watched *Shrek 2*, again. When it finished, I happened to pick up Mum's holiday brochure. I opened it. The first picture I saw was of an orang-utan gazing out at me, wide-eyed and thoughtful. There flashed through my mind then a most dreadful image. I must have seen it on television, or maybe from a nature magazine, most likely the *National Geographic* – we had a pile of them in the bathroom at home. It was a photograph of a terrified young orang-utan clinging pathetically to the top of a charred tree, the forest all around burnt to the ground. I turned the page quickly, not wanting to be reminded of it any more. That was when I came across the picture of an elephant walking along a beach, and being ridden by a boy no older than I was. I could not contain my excitement. 'Mum,' I said, 'look at this! They've got elephants, and you can ride them!' But Mum was fast asleep, and showing no signs whatever of wanting to wake up.

Some of the people in the brochure looked a lot like Mum, I noticed. She never talked to me about Indonesia that much, but I'd always known that was where her family had come from originally. She was Swiss as well, which was why we'd been over there a few times, to see my other grandparents. 'Licorice Allsort', that's what Dad used to call me: 'Bit Indonesian, bit Swiss, and a bit Scottish, like me. Best of all worlds, that's what you are, Will,' he'd say. I'd always been very proud of having a mother who didn't look much like my friends' mothers. Her skin was honey brown, smooth and soft, and she had shining black hair. I would have preferred to look like her, but I'm much more like my father – sort of pinkish, with a thatch of thick fair hair, 'like ripe corn', Grandpa called it.

I couldn't help myself. It was something I'd been doing a lot. I kept trying to picture Dad as he was when I last saw him, but all that came into my head was the photo of him I remembered best, the one on top of the piano with him holding the pike. I knew that a memory of a photo isn't a real memory at all. I promised myself again that I would think about Dad more often, however much it hurt me. How else could I keep in touch with him? I wanted to see his smile again, to hear how his voice sounded. Remembering him was the only way. It worried me that, if I didn't remember him often, then maybe one day I'd forget him altogether. I needed to remember, but then it troubled me when I did. It was troubling me now, which was why I turned my attention again to the holiday brochure. On every page there seemed to be more elephants. Elephants, I decided, were quite definitely supreme.

And now here I was actually riding one along a beach. I couldn't believe it. I wished then I had Mum's mobile phone on me. I longed to ring Grandpa and tell him what I was doing. I said out loud the first words that came into my head. 'You're not going to believe this, Grandpa!' I held my arms high, lifted my face towards the sun, and whooped with joy. The *mahout* turned round and laughed aloud with me.

I think I've loved elephants ever since I was little, probably ever since my first Babar book. Best of all I loved the story of the Elephant's Child, whose nose had been tugged and tugged, until it was stretched into a proper trunk by a crocodile, down by 'the great grey green greasy Limpopo River, all hung about with fever trees'. Grandpa had read it to me so often at bedtimes that I knew some of it by heart. Ever since then, I've always loved any natural history programme, just so long as there are elephants in it. And now I was in one, on one, and in my own programme! I whooped again, punching the air. High above me, probably at about 35,000 feet, I thought, flew a silver dart of a plane, its vapour trail long and straight.

'I was up there,' I told the *mahout*. But he didn't seem to be listening. He was looking out to sea. He seemed distracted by something. So I told Oona instead. 'I was up there with Mum,' I told her, 'in a plane just like that one. And there was an elephant just like you, in the brochure. Maybe it was you.'

I remembered how, when Mum woke up, she leant over me, brushing my hair away from my eyes. 'I should have cut your hair at Grandma's,' she said. 'I'll do it when we get to the hotel. It's too long. You look like a right ragamuffin.'

'Mum,' I told her, fixing her with my most determined look. 'When we get there, I'm not going to waste time having a stupid haircut, am I? You know what I'm going to do? I'm going to go for a ride on an elephant.' I showed her the brochure. 'Look at that!'

'Are they safe?'

'Course they are, Mum. Can I?'

'We'll see,' she said. 'I expect it'll be a bit expensive. We'll have to watch our pennies, you know.'

The hotel was right on the beach, and just as beautiful as it had looked in the brochure. And there was an elephant, too, we were told, which sometimes gave hour-long rides all the way down the beach and back. Every day I looked out for this elephant, but much to my disappointment it was never there. There were compensations enough, though. We spent an entire week messing around on the beach, swimming and snorkelling. It was a week filled with endless sun and fun, all in all the very best kind of forgetting. Then on Christmas day, Mum told me I wasn't getting a Christmas present this year, I was going to have an elephant ride instead. She'd arranged the whole thing, for the next day, for Boxing Day.

So that's how come, on Boxing Day, I found myself sitting there high up on an elephant, on a kind of cushioned throne – Mum said she thought it was called a howdah, or something that sounded like it, anyway. There was a wooden rail all around to hold onto. But when the elephant set off, the ride was so smooth that I found I didn't need to hold on at all. I rode along the beach on my throne, looking down on the world around me. I felt like a king up there, or an emperor maybe, or a sultan, except that Mum did rather spoil the illusion by trotting alongside taking photos of me on her phone to send home to Grandma and Grandpa. I acted up for the camera, waving at it, regally. 'Hi Grandpa, hi Grandma. King Will here. What d'you think of my new tractor then, Grandpa?' I shouted all sorts of nonsense. This was better than I had ever imagined. I felt on top of the world.

'Happy up there, Your Majesty?' Mum said, beaming up at me.

'S'all right, I suppose,' I told her.

'Mind you keep your hat on, Will, and your shirt. Don't want you getting sunstroke or sunburn, do we?' She went on and on and on. 'And you've got the sun cream, and that bottle of water I gave you, haven't you? It's hot, and it'll get hotter.'

'Yes, Mum. I'll be all right, Mum.' I was trying to make light of my irritation. 'I'll be fine. Honest, Mum. See you when I get back.'

'Don't fall off,' she called after me. 'Hang on tight. It's a long way down. You will be all right up there, won't you?'

I didn't like her fussing me, and especially not in front of the *mahout*. I waved her goodbye, waving her away at the same time. 'Don't worry, Mum,' I told her. 'You go and have a swim. It's brill, Mum, just brill.' And it was true. I'd never had a ride as brilliant as this, nor as easy as this, nor as high as this. I remembered the donkey on the beach at Weston-super-Mare, with its jerky little steps; and Minky, the Haflinger horse I'd ridden once in Guarda in Switzerland, who used to break into a sudden trot whenever she felt like it, who bumped me up and down in the saddle so hard I couldn't sit down afterwards. This elephant was slow, gentle, dignified. Whatever she had for shock absorbers was fantastic. All I had to do was move with her, sway with her rhythm, and that was as easy as pie. It felt almost as if I was afloat. Riding an elephant seemed as natural to me as breathing.

I'd been so wrapped up in my own thoughts, so enthralled by the elephant, and by everything around me, that only now did I think of Mum. I swivelled around in my howdah to look for her. I could see there were dozens of swimmers in the sea just below the hotel. I tried to spot her red bikini, or the light blue sarong that Dad had given her, but we'd gone a long way away from them by now, and I couldn't pick her out from among the others. The sea was so still now, it seemed almost unreal. It seemed to me as if it was breathing in, then holding its breath waiting for something to happen, something fearful. It made me feel suddenly anxious too, which was why I kept turning round now, looking for Mum. I still couldn't see her. I began to feel myself being gripped by a rising panic. I didn't know why, but all I wanted to do was to go back. I wanted to be with her. I had to be sure she was safe.

That was the moment Oona stopped, without any warning at all. She was looking out to sea, her whole body tensed. She was breathing hard, short sharp breaths. Then she lifted her trunk and began trumpeting at the sea, tossing her head as if there was something out there, something that terrified her. The *mahout* was trying to calm her, but she wasn't paying him any attention.

I looked out to sea then, and noticed that the horizon had changed. It looked as if a white line had been drawn across it, separating sea from sky. As I watched I could see that this line was moving ever closer towards us, that the sea was being sucked away, leaving hundreds of fish floundering on the sand. Oona swung round and, before the *mahout* could stop her, she was running towards the trees. In those first few hurried strides I very nearly fell off. I managed to stay on, only by clinging on tight with both hands to the rail in front of me. I held on for dear life, as Oona stampeded up the beach, and into the shadows of the jungle.

Afterword

TEN PAIRS OF GRUBBY FEET are so tightly jammed together it's difficult to tell brother from sister, child from grandchild. Ten huddled bodies sound asleep inside a makeshift shelter that is barely big enough to house them. Saplings, crudely cut, provide the walls. Dried grass and leaves form a patchwork roof. The crowning glory – the precious, donated plastic sheeting – is stretched to its limit across the top. If it doesn't rain too hard, it should hold.

Seraphine inches along the narrow corridor of unoccupied floor towards the cloth-covered entrance of her tiny wooden shelter. When the children wake they will need water. It's what will keep them alive. It's what Oxfam will provide.

Seraphine is forty-two years old: a mother and a grandmother. The children are all she has. Her home, her possessions, many of her friends and neighbours, are gone. Her husband is dead – shot as the family ran. To the south, away from the fighting. To Goma, capital city of the troubled Democratic Republic of Congo. To Mugunga, a sprawling settlement of some 18,000 people.

It's not home, but it's somewhere to call home. Somewhere to draw breath, grieve, look for hope. Seraphine has to stay strong. She is now sole carer and lone provider for her traumatised family. Getting to Mugunga camp was her first test. Here, there are people who can help. Organisations that can provide food, blankets, soap, medicine and, critically, water.

Supplying water to Mugunga, and three other nearby camps, has been a massive undertaking for Oxfam. The desolate and unforgiving terrain is formed from hard-as-nails volcanic rocks. Digging for boreholes was out of the question. Finding a way to pump water from Lake Kivu, some two and a half miles away, was the only option. And it had to be done fast.

The rhythmic chug-chug-chug of a diesel-driven waterpump is now a faint, but familiar, sound to thousands of people living in the camps. Along with a second pump, submerged deep beneath the lake, it pushes water through wide plastic pipes to storage tanks and tapstands.

Snaking across rocks and through mud, this network of over-ground tubing really is a lifeline. Without a steady supply of clean water, without decent sanitation, waterborne diseases could sweep through the camps with devastating results. Dehydration, diarrhoea, cholera. All three are death sentences for people who are already undernourished and whose immune systems are too weak to put up a fight.

Seraphine's day starts early – just after 5 a.m. Another fifty-three minutes and the sun will rise along with the temperature. When she reaches the nearest tapstand, just minutes from her hut, Seraphine knows that the water will be there. She can turn on a tap and fill her jerry can whenever she needs water to cook with, to wash with, to drink – to keep her children clean and disease at bay. In Mugunga there are 18,000 more

Seraphines, and the task of ensuring a constant supply of clean water to so many people is a daily challenge. Collaboration is vital. Training, and involving the men and women who live in the camps, is what will keep the water flowing. Everyone has a role to play. In Mugunga, volunteers learn how to test chlorine levels, help to spread the message about good hygiene, dig latrines, unload supplies. And when Oxfam moves on to the next emergency, our local partners will keep everything going for as long as they are needed.

Many of the world's emergencies are the direct result of prolonged and continuing conflict: Sudan, Somalia, Chad, Afghanistan, the Democratic Republic of Congo to name just a few. But even if, by some miracle of political will, the world managed to put an end to all wars tomorrow, so-called natural disasters would still keep us busy. Floods, famine, drought, hurricanes, earthquakes. They are becoming more frequent, more prolonged. Climate change is a major factor. Disasters are surely more man-made than natural as the world's ever-increasing population pumps more and more carbon into the environment and strips our planet of fuel and forests. It is poor communities that are suffering. And when disaster does strike, Oxfam is there – supplying clean water and sanitation.

But it's not all rapid response. Oxfam also works with hundreds of communities around the world that need water for their fields, for their animals, for everyday use. This takes a more considered approach and can yield some amazing results. Water – captured, contained and delivered in the right way – will help people to grow what they need and more. Food on the table, with enough left over to sell at the local market, is a prize worth having. A modest income can pay for medicines, school books, clothes. Every community has its own challenges. And its own innovative solutions.

In north-east Brazil hundreds of concrete water tanks are now a familiar sight across the arid landscape. It's one of the most drought-prone regions of the country and if you live here you get used to eating dust. Mile after mile of khaki-coloured soil that is blown in all directions by the slightest movement, by the mildest winds. But it is here in this seeming dustbowl where Oxfam – working with local partner, Diaconia – is helping families to grow fruit and vegetables in abundance. Paulo Lopez is proud of the two large tanks he helped to build. They catch and store the rainwater that falls for just three months of each year. The amount and abundance of fruit and vegetables in Paulo's garden is nothing short of a miracle. Passion fruit, papaya, mangoes, bananas, pomegranates, tomatoes, oranges and lemons, now grow from once-parched soil.

With enough water, anything and everything is possible. It's all too easy to forget what a miracle water is. Until it's not there. On tap, at our fingertips. People in developing countries don't take water for granted. Too much can be as disastrous as too little. Oxfam works with thousands of communities to get the balance right. Your support is vital.

oxfam.org.uk/emergencies

Oxfam

Be Humankind